A Voice In The Rain

Book Two of
The Storm Tales

G.W. "TABBI" DORSEY

Book Two of
The Storm Tales

A Voice in the Rain
Copyright © 2017 G. W. "Tabbi" Dorsey
For Epiphany Productions

ISBN: 978-1-5356-1521-1

Dedication

This book is dedicated to those in need of a rainbow to signal the ending of the storm. Those looking for encouragement and closure after a sudden lost. Those seeking permission to grieve and then move on. This book is a continuation of a story that began as an outlet for all those living in fear and pain while attempting to suffer quietly. This book is meant to be your voice, so that after your many years of trying to recover from your struggles with little or no success, you will suddenly arrive at that place of realization. You will realize that all the experiences in life serve not only to shape us into who we are, but prepare us for what is yet to come.

A thought to ponder in the days ahead:

"Practice breeds perfection, so if you do something well continue; If you make a mistake, don't repeat it."

Reviews

"I swelled for Dee and Sky. I found this author's language usage refreshingly gripping and before I realized it, I was taken in by the characterization of these siblings and caught up in the epic saga of their fear-fettered lives."

~C. J. Bland, Avid reader

"Book Two of The Storm Tales has a level of intensity that keeps you on the edge of your seat for the entire book. It's like the most extreme roller coaster ride ever. I love the way Ms. Dorsey keeps you guessing, but just like in book one she clearly delivers."

~Rayne, Counselor

"I would like to express my admiration and appreciation to the author of The Storm Tales Trilogy! She has managed to bring to the forefront a very important issue concerning today's society and does it in such a way as to enlighten without bombarding you. I fell in love with some characters and rooted against others, but all in all I couldn't turn pages fast enough to see what was going to happen next! Each book draws you in more and more, so I wait anxiously for Book Three with mixed feelings; the greatest of which is anticipation. I know you will enjoy these books as much as I did!"

~Roslyn, Administrative Assistant

"I crave an opportunity to conversate with a woman that can render me speechless with her words. Ms. Duggan's writing style does not capture because you will graciously surrender and beg for the next book. Purchasing kneepads before I finish this one because I will be waiting with baited breath for book three."

~A. Johnson, housewife.

"I'M NOT MUCH OF A READER BUT I FOUND MYSELF CAUGHT UP IN THE CHARACTERS AND THE STRUGGLES THEY ENDURED AND ALSO THEIR JOY'S***** G.W. DUGGAN IS A VERY PASSIONATE AND ACCOMPLISHED WRITER AS WELL AS A GREAT PERSON WHO'S OVERCOME MANY OBSTACLES IN HER OWN LIFE TO BECOME THE BEAUTIFUL YET STRONG WOMAN OF POWER I'VE COME TO KNOW AND RESPECT~ "

~Q. Readdy

Table of Contents

Prologue...

Beginning of the End

We all know that there are no true endings, only new beginnings. When first we met the Stephens children, they were trying desperately to progress through a traumatic childhood.

Here we find them learning to overcome the trials of adolescence to become healthy functioning adults. Trying to live normal lives with normal interactions with those around them. Attempting to have what they were never allowed to have before.

Libby was instrumental in guiding them through the difficult times and giving them solace in the rough times and now here they have arrived at adulthood and we find that very little has changed for them. Except for the loss of the one thing that they never wanted to be without, a sudden ending to the part of their lives that they wished would have gone on forever.

They find themselves with questions and no answers, in a shower of confusion with no shelter in sight. They must remember that there is something that they can always depend on, the love from one that will always be there. But they learn this powerful lesson after many years of grief.

What happens when someone you love dies? What happens to the time that you spent with them? What does your life become when the person that made you what you are leaves you? Questions will always arise. The problem is what happens when there is no one you trust to give you answers.

What happens when a stranger becomes everything to you, someone that does not have to love you but does anyway? Someone that fills up a void in your life that you never even knew existed. A person that makes you whole when you didn't even know you were in pieces. The person that gives you all the things that you are missing before you realize that they were gone. Libby was this person for me; she was mother, a friend, a guide, my support, my encouragement, an honest resource, true entertainment and real protection. Simply, Libby was love. Something I barely knew anything about, but desperately wanted. A force in my life to provide me with what every little girl wants, needs and should never be without.

Libby brought so much into our lives that we were lacking, that we often wondered how we survived before she came. Yes, along with Libby came Charles but, life must have balance; so there will always be some clouds in the sky even when we have the sun.

Libby was the rain that falls from the clouds and washes everything and helps maintain and restore life. Charles was the thunder and lightning that reminds us to respect nature and never ignore the warnings of a pending storm.

Chapter One...

There Is Always More to Tell

M aria found herself sitting in a waiting room with people she would ordinarily have nothing in common with. People waiting to visit an inmate in the state prison system. Why was she here, why did she feel compelled to visit a man that by right she should hate?

Maria was here because she needed the truth. Maria had been told the police version from their evidence, she had sat thru a trying monologue from Libby, she had even tried to listen to the blubbering version of Dee's story about that day at the tree house.

Maria had even tried to accept the rational version given to her by her loving husband. Surprise of all surprises, that Dr. Chase had managed to convince her to marry him. In doing so, Montgomery had worked hard to also convince her that she needed love in her life and someone to take care of her.

As they stood on the beach outside their condo and exchanged their wedding vows, Maria knew that all the arguments that he had made for them getting married were valid, but she was not certain it was the right thing to do.

She had married Montgomery anyway and told herself it was because it made him happy and she felt that she owed him that after all the years of therapy he had given her.

Maria knew that Montgomery would not be happy to know that she felt that way, he also would not be happy to know that she was here waiting to see Charles. But Maria needed something even her picture-perfect life with Montgomery could not give her, she needed the truth.

Even after all the conversations, a few of which that skirted argument territory; Maria knew that the only version of the truth that would quiet the mental beast raging inside her head, would have to come from the beast itself. She needed the one she had never been able to get until now.

The only person that had not spoken, was the one person she was desperate to hear from, Charles himself. For some reason beyond normal sanity Maria needed to speak with Charles face to face, to ask the questions that had lived in her head and heart all these years.

The questions that dominated her waking hours, consistently marched through her dreams and monopolized her therapy sessions.

Amazing that after marrying her therapist, she still required those weekly sessions to keep her balanced. Too bad she had had to find another therapist. Too bad also that she was told the same things by the new therapist that Montgomery had told her. Had given her the same answers.

Because none of the answers she had been given made sense, none of the reasons felt right; here she sat waiting to finally see Charles. After many years of denials and refusals by him to even accept her letters, she would hopefully find what she sought.

Charles never expected to find himself here, but was not surprised that this is where his life had lead him. Libby had often told him in those last months that he should mind his thoughts lest they lead him somewhere he did not wish to be. As always, he could rely on the truth of Libby's words, for here he was. Somewhere he most definitely did not want to be.

4

Most people would think that prison would be the worst place on earth for a man like him, but right now there was something he feared even more than being a convicted and confessed child molester in prison; that was sitting across the table from the woman walking toward him for a single second let alone an hour.

What had he been thinking when he agreed to let Maria visit him. For years he had refused her requests, returned her letters and denied her appeals through his attorney. But Libby always told him that one must answer for their mistakes and speak the truth when faced with questions regarding their wrongs.

As Charles watched Maria plop down in the chair across from him, he knew this was exactly what Libby had been speaking about. The question in his mind was not why was she here, but would he answer her questions; and if so would he answer honestly.

Maria sat there waiting for Charles to say something. He had to know why she was here surely, he did not think that she was here just for a visit. He sat there looking at her like he wanted her to say something.

Maria knew what she wanted to know and at the same time she was afraid of the answers she might receive if she asked those dreaded questions. Truthfully, she could not think of a way to ask the questions she wanted answers to. In her mind that voice said, just do it. But could she. Could she really ask him the questions that she had been posing to her therapist and to herself for all those years.

Finally, she realized if she did not ask, it would continue to haunt her and invade every area of her life and control her every waking moment. So, Maria asked the question. She asked Charles was it his plan from the beginning, was his whole reason for all he had done was just so he could have his way with her daughter. After voicing it, Maria realized that there was relief in just having spoken the words. Even without his response, there was a release of breath she did not even remember holding.

Charles just sat there looking at her like he had never seen her before. Charles did exactly what she expected him to do, nothing. He just sat there looking at her. Maria decided that she would sit there as long as she had to in order to get the answers she wanted. No, the answers she needed. If she was ever going to have any peace in her life, ever going to have calm in her mind she needed answers. So, she would wait.

Maria had spent so many years asking questions, in the end that's all she had was questions. Why had she not seen the truth of what Charles was, even back in college she did not let herself see him for who he really was. How did she not know that her ex-husband was a monster that would take everything that mattered to her and shred it to a pile of broken pieces. The little hints of temper were there when they were dating and she told herself she needed to be calm and less jealous.

Another question that haunted her, was when did her sister become such a self-absorbed narcissist that cared only for her own happiness and no one else mattered as much as she did, or had she always been that way and Maria missed it because she loved her sister and would have accepted anything Ashley offered.

Maria had an answer to one question that had been asked of her and there was no doubt about the love she had for her son. The truth of that was in the fact that she and Sky had been the only ones in the kitchen and only they knew that she had been too far away to prevent him from shooting Charles that day.

But given the choice of letting her son be punished for an action that by right she should have taken and lying about what really happened that day, she had admitted responsibility for the shooting; or at least muddied the water so it was not clear who really did it.

Now sitting here staring at Charles across the table waiting for him to say something, Maria realized that maybe Charles knew the truth as well as she did and wondered why he had never told anyone. More questions to add to the long laundry list that lived within her already.

Maria began to ask herself if that was why Charles had really been refusing all forms of contact with her. Could it have been that he knew the truth all along. That even though Sky had pulled the trigger, it was what she had wanted to do and he did not want to give her another chance to finish what had been started that day in the kitchen so long ago.

Maybe if this visit did not go well, the real truth would finally see the light of day. After all, that is what Libby would say. She would say that everything done in the dark, will come to the light. Surely, he would want people to know the truth about her and her children. But the truth of the matter is, that everyone should know either way by now.

The other question was, did she really care. The answer to that one was that she did not care. Of all the questions that she wanted answers to, this was one that she really could care less about. Maria was willing to wait to get what she wanted and do what she needed to do to get it.

Charles had never wanted any of this to happen. Truthfully, he had not expected anyone to believe Dee as he had told her back in the tree house.

Obviously, more people paid attention than he realized because here he sat. Held in protective custody to keep the other inmates from carrying out their threats to end his life painfully and slowly.

Honestly in his mind, he felt that he had done nothing wrong. He had been merely helping the daughter of a friend. But it had been difficult to explain that to his cellmates, who thought he was a crazed animal that needed to be put down.

Which explained his frequent arrivals to the infirmary and the emergency room after multiple violent attacks. Several of which had been very near fatal, like the seven stab wounds which had cost him a kidney. The fall down the stairs that led to a severe concussion and three weeks in a medically induced coma to allow his brain to stop swelling. He had experienced four broken noses and a shattered left knee which required him to use a cane. A clavicle that had been fractured twice and now refused to heal a third time. All these things passed through his mind as he sat and stared at the woman that he had once called friend for more than twenty years.

Chapter Two...

Letting Go of Lost Causes

Bradley sat staring out the window waiting for his sister to come give him a ride home. He had seen the therapist for training to learn how to maneuver a wheelchair with 4 broken ribs and a broken leg that ached like a toothache.

He had listened with quiet rage to the strange man that came and informed him that the only way he could stay out of jail was to attend 12 weeks of intense Anger Management therapy. He would go but he did not expect to get anything out of it, he wasn't the one that started all this. His problems began at a high school dance that had left him with more than a metal plated jaw. He now had a gut full of rage for a man that probably cared less if he still lived and breathed.

Because he could not take his anger and frustration out on his true target anyone else would do. He cared very little who found themselves on the other end of his fists or feet, he just needed someone to aim at.

This time it had been three drunk guys in a bar talking to a woman he could care less about. He did not even remember her name if he ever even knew it, she was an end to a means and that was all. He had been fired from his job, again. This time for getting in his boss's face about what, he could not remember. Then he had gone to the local bar where he knew bar fights were as routine as the city church bells chiming at twelve noon on Sunday.

So here he sat in the hospital, again, waiting for Melody (Mel as he like to call her) to come and take him home. He knew she would be angry, but at least this time she would not miss work. Mel told him she would be there after her shift ended around 4:30 so he would sit and wait. Wait for Mel to show up with that sad, angry disappointed look on her face; and wait for the pain pill the nurse had given him to kick in and dull some of the many aches and pains he was feeling. He was amazed that he got any relief at all considering what his body had been through over the years.

Between the injuries from just not paying attention and the many fights, he had spent half his trust fund on bail, medical bills and pain medication.

As Mel entered the room and angrily asked, "Are you ready to go?" Bradley thought her voice should have had some compassion in it considering it was coming from someone that worked around sick people, but his sister had long since lost any sympathy or compassion for him after so many trips to the hospital and the police station.

He knew the one and only thing she would say when she got him in the truck, "You really need to get some help and get your life together before you kill yourself or someone else does it for you."

As Mel loaded him and then his wheelchair in the truck she was quiet. Waiting, Bradley thought till they were driving. As Mel drove through town, she said nothing. As she was cut off twice on the freeway, she said nothing. That actually caught Bradley's attention because for such a petite woman, she had a mountain sized case of road rage. The only thing that rivaled his younger sister's road rage was his rage at everything and everyone.

When they arrived at his condo and Mel still had not made her token statement, Bradley thought maybe she was just too tired from work to trifle with him, but there was more to this story and he was so not ready for the ending.

As Melody helped him maneuver up the ramp and then to the door, it was then he noticed the difference because he could see her reflection clearly in the glass. Her face was set in an expression he had never seen before, so somehow he knew this talk would be different.

As they exited the elevator he almost hesitated rolling down the hall, because now he could actually feel the difference in Melody. There was a set to her shoulders and even her steps were different as she walked down the hall. Bradley sat there watching as she opened the door to his condo thinking is this what it feels like to be lead to the gallows. Instead of going in ahead of him, Mel pushed the door open, and stepped aside for him to enter. He rolled inside and turned around to ask her if she would like to stay and order Chinese, but the words as well as the taste for food of any kind died a horrible death as he saw the silent tears rolling down his sister's face.

He was about to tell her that he was not hurt that bad, but she started speaking first. She told him that she could no longer keep coming to his rescue. That this was his last ride home from the hospital or the police station with her. When he tried to offer an apology she simply held up her hand and said, "Save it Bradley. Because you are not going to stop until you die, like you almost did all those years ago and maybe it would have been better than this slow suicide route you are taking now but I won't ride with you anymore." Mel did not even look him in the face, as she said her last words. "Find someone else to watch you bleed your life away. You are the only family I have left and I love you, but I am done. Goodbye and good luck." Mel laid Bradley's keys on the table and softly closed the door as she left. He wished she had slammed it, maybe it would have hurt less.

He had known his sister would be angry with him but he had no idea that he could lose her. Now what, who would he call? Who would tell him to get his life together? How would he get to his appointments, how would he get to the store, the bank and all those other places?

The strange man that he was visited by before he left the hospital had told him that he would need to think about what he wanted his life to be. Bradley already knew that, had known since what he had wanted most, walked into the gym wearing a pair of blue volleyball shorts. Not the really short ones that most of the girls wore, but a pair that fit nice and left a lot to the imagination. Something about the fact that he could not see if she did or did not wear underwear. Just the fact that he could not make out the true shape of her body made him pay more attention. He had wanted DeTalia Yvonne Stephens. He wanted his life to be what it had been before that fateful day in the gym.

No one knew how much he hated Skylur Stephens. If only he had never met him his life would be so different. Not to mention that he would have a totally different life if he had been allowed to be with Detalia the way he wanted, they would be together and happy now. He believed that he was the perfect man for her and she would have come to that understanding as well if only her brother had not gotten involved in their relationship.

Maybe once he was well enough to drive he would go look for Dee and tell her that he had never stopped thinking of her and that he still wanted to be with her even though he could not stand her brother and wished him dead. A minor detail he thought it best not to share with Dee.

Chapter Three...

The Truth is Never Obvious

Vanni had no idea how he had arrived at this place. His routine of running every morning had always been a joy. One that he was glad to have because it allowed him time to think, to reflect and plan. It was also his time to pray. Praying was something that had never been a part of routine before, not even his life before Libby. It was one of the things that he had loved most about her, that she had a way of helping you change before you even realized that something needed to be changed.

Vanni would give much to have Libby right now to help him figure out his current situation and change it. He thought he was living his best life yet. He had four beautiful children, a wife that was everything he could ever ask for and so much more. He loved the ranch and so glad that they had moved here from the city to raise their children and be around the animals that they all loved. He even enjoyed having Sky right across the lake because it gave Dee the peace of being close to her brother. So what had gone wrong? He could never recall a time when he and Dee were not completely in sync with each other. Even when the children were having moments of temporary insanity and his mother in law was having Bipolar episodes, life at home was great because he had the love of his life. Somehow something had gone very wrong and they had experienced their very first argument and he felt like his heart had been put through a meat grinder. The things that he had said were harsh and now that he replayed them in his mind, he realized they were wrong; he was wrong.

Out here in the morning air halfway through his run, the truth came softly like one of Libby's cream puffs. But the weight of it hit like his old sparring partner and he knew that the bruises would be there for a while. Now the treatment, he had to get home and tell Dee that he understood and that he knew why those ugly questions had come to her mind. He knew the real reason just as sure as if Libby had told him herself and maybe she had. This was about to be the fastest 2 miles back he had ever run.

How did this happen, Dee and Vanni had just woken up the morning after their first real argument and for the life of her she could not remember what had even caused it. It had been a beautiful Saturday morning and she wanted to go for a walk by the lake. The children were out with the animals and trying to get their uncle Sky to teach them his favorite magic trick. Vanni began his Saturday morning like always, 2 hours in the gym, then his run. He had a magnificent body and Dee knew how he kept it that way. 2 hours in the gym 5 days a week, 5 mile runs every day of the week. He never skipped breakfast with the children and he always had his morning snuggle with her and then off to the gym that he had added onto the ranch after their marriage to maintain that body that would threaten any Greek gods' title.

Somewhere between their morning snuggle and helping Angel start lunch, all Hell broke loose.

There was no rhyme or reason to it, she had simply asked an honest question and he had gotten offended. Come to think of it, she really couldn't fathom what made her ask the question in the first place. Looking back on it now, it almost seems as if the argument had been her prime directive and sole purpose for asking him that awful question. A simple question really, but a question that had turned her entire world upside down. Her question had been, "had he really just married her out of pity?"

Where had that thought even come from, there was no basis for it and she had never felt anything to suggest that pity might have even the smallest place in her marriage. What was happening to her, was she becoming her mother or was she in real need of all that therapy that had been ordered for her as a child.

As Dee stood in the shower staring blankly at the tile, she continued to replay the scene in her head. What had triggered such an ugly thought, and why ever did she let it fall out of her mouth.

She saw no more reason for it now than she did last night as she lay crying herself to sleep, while Vanni was somewhere in the house other than where he belonged lying spoon fashion with her.

After much back and forth Dee began to pull herself together and decided she simply had to find Vanni and tell him that she had finally lost her mind. But just to make sure she did it right, because there is a right way and a wrong to tell your husband that you have gone insane; she would call Libby and talk to her first.

Just as she walked over to the phone and began dialing she remembered that Libby was gone and that she would never be able to get that motherly advice or be held in the arms of true unconditional love ever again. She slid to the floor in uncontrollable sobs and hiccups that were very much like the ones she often shed as a child in Libby's lap for one reason or another.

That's where Vanni found her in a puddle on the floor by their bed, still cradling the phone. Vanni forgot everything except his desperate love for this woman that was still so much a child. He knew at the sight of the phone she held with a deathly grip what had happened. He knew because of all the times he had found her just this way right after Libby's passing.

He did the only thing he could do, he held her, rocked her gently and loved her more than ever before. Vanni had realized what the whole ordeal last night was about, and could have round-housed himself in the head for not seeing it sooner. His precious womanchild was afraid. Afraid of losing him as she had already lost so much. He could not promise never to leave her, but he damn well would make her feel safe while he was here.

The anger he felt for having lashed out at her about her question and his stupidity at not realizing its cause made him shed tears of his own. His mother had been right all those years ago when she had said that men are stupid sometimes.

After prying the phone out of her grip, Vanni lifted Dee to the bed they had shared every night of their marriage, except last night when he had fallen asleep in Libby's rocker. He vowed on all his love for Libby, last night would be the first and last night that she would sleep and obviously by the smell of her tears still in the sheets, cry alone in their bed if he could help it.

He rolled Dee over on his chest, so he could look into those eyes that held him captive every time he saw them. For the first time ever, he did not allow her to speak first but told her everything that was in his heart, much of which she had heard many times before but also a few things she had not.

They made love as if it were their wedding night all over again, but this time without any hesitation on either one's part.

Dee awoke later cuddled in Vanni's embrace and although she had woken up in this exact place many times before, something about this time was very different. Dee knew the pain and fear first hand that comes from losing one of the most important things in your life. Not since Libby's death had she hurt so much and been so afraid. This type of fear had been commonplace in her childhood, but she had managed to escape it in her adult life, or so she thought. It was an ugly way to find out that some things never go away, they become a part of your life and they never leave you.

16

After their marriage Dee and Vanni quickly realized that they were more comfortable at the ranch than they were anywhere else. Strange how even though some awful things had happened here, more of her life's happy memories had happened at the ranch than sad. So they decided that's where they wanted to live and raise their children.

For years Libby had kept the chains of fear from choking the happiness completely out of her life and now that Libby was gone Dee would have to find a way to keep the monster under the bed and the boogeyman in the closet all on her own. Living here at the ranch helped to keep Dee near Libby and her memories, it also kept the nightmares at bay. Then just before she fell asleep the answer came softly as if Libby had whispered it to her, your faith is the key.

So as Dee gave into the peaceful sleep that comes with happiness and being safe and truly loved, she decided that her family would do what her parents never did, love God and each other always for God was the answer to every question.

Chapter Four...

The Silent Monster Within

S ky lay in bed staring at the beautiful vaulted ceiling that he and Mina had restored. His mind continued to replay the afternoon that they had worked on this very room. The day had started with them trying to decide the color of the paint and trim for the room. He had wanted antique white and powder blue because the light colors were the opposite of the rooms in his childhood home. Mina had wanted Sunshine yellow walls with white trim, because it reminded her of a kitchen from her past.

They ended up with a powder blue room, trimmed in antique white with yellow box trim around the whole room. Mina said it was called compromise, something he was beginning to understand more being with her.

But only because he wanted to continue being with her, not because he believed it really worked. But then Sky was not one for believing in much of anything.

There was one thing that Sky knew with absolute certainty and that was that all things happened for a reason. This was something that he had learned from Libby and one of the only things that he had held on to from all that she had told him all those years ago when he spent his weekends at the ranch in her kitchen.

Sky now knew that he and his sister had had to go through hell for a reason. What that reason was, had not yet made itself apparent but it would. The other grand entrance that he waited for was the reason for Mina back in his life. He knew three things for certain, he was calmer when she was near. Sometimes just thinking about her relaxed him. Mina seemed to understand him and never pushed him and the most important thing that had revealed itself to him was the one thing he feared most. The knowledge that he never wanted to be without her, the fact that he loved her.

As Sky lay thinking about the realization that he was in love with Mina, he tried to figure out how this had happened.

When did he cross that line that he had drawn for himself years ago. Had it happened when he used to read to her and the other children while spending time at the hospital waiting for his mother to get better and come home. Was that when it really started, because truth be told even then she had a calming and positive effect on him.

He stood and walked to the window. As he stared out at the rock garden that he and Mina had taken two months to build he asked himself what was he to do now?

What do you do when you find yourself in a place you never wanted to be and never thought you would be; in love. He asked himself what did that really mean, because if he followed the example set by his parents; then he knew it was one of the worst things on earth to have happen to you. So, he had to ask himself could he actually be in love? And if so, what did this thing call love feel like?

If it was like what he felt when he was at the ranch with his sister's family and the animals then it was playful, entertaining and comfortable. If it was more like what he felt when he was working on restoring an old house; then it was focused, intense and totally engaging.

But truthfully none of those really compared to what he felt when he was with Mina. With her there was calm, peace and a warmth that he had never experienced before.

When she looked at him or smiled at him there was a tightening in his chest that felt like nothing on earth. But there was no fear, no pain and no anger. Mina made him feel things he swore he would never need or want beyond what he had with his family. But yet, here he stood pondering those very things.

All his life his anger had felt like hot lava boiling deep inside him and it just waited for any opportunity to spill out and destroy anything in its path. Mina had a way of not just cooling his anger but erasing it all together like it was never there. But could he trust something that he had so very little knowledge and experience with. Sky did not trust feelings and emotions, he had seen the damage that could result when you acted on feelings and he did not enjoy it one bit.

Sky's perusal of his list of reasons to distrust his feelings was interrupted by the ringing of the phone, something else he did not enjoy.

Sky relaxed when he heard the deep timbre of Martin Garvey's voice. He went from feeling apprehensive to curious as he offered his appropriate responses to Garvey and listened to Garvey explain the purpose of his call. Never one to mince words or beat around the bush as it were, he made talking to him simple and easy. All you had to do was listen and then agree or disagree. Sky of course agreed to be at the prearranged meeting to assist Garvey with a new problem that had been dropped in his lap. They said their goodbyes and hung up. Now Sky had a whole new focus, something that did not require him to feel just remember.

Sky sat again staring at the rock garden and reminisced about his initial meeting with Martin Luther Garvey. Garvey was the owner and lead counselor at a place called *Resolution Counseling & Therapy Group*. *Resolution* was a place to get the help that people really needed with anger, bad attitudes and other behaviors that could lead to being arrested, prison time or death.

The man stood six feet six and was built like a linebacker carved from a solid brick wall. He was the largest black man Sky had ever seen and with a smile that could instill more fear than any frown even Freddy Kruger could conjure up.

At their first meeting Sky just knew that there were some witches that never wanted to hear the name Martin Luther Garvey because even they would be afraid of him.

Garvey as he was called, was named by his mother who was a political activist that loved Martin Luther King, Jr and was rumored to be a faithful participant in civil rights activities.

Garvey was the type of man that emitted strength in every possible way. His only potential weakness was a missing left hand, which he never explained and not even the devil himself would ask what had happened to it.

Sky had been introduced to Mr. Garvey after his fight in the gym with Bradley Garrison. Lt. Alexander had taken Sky to meet him and explained that it would help Sky avoid some difficulties later.

Garvey was the one that explained that by Sky taking anger management therapy at *Resolution* it would look better and hopefully prevent him from being criminally charged over his actions regarding Bradley. That and his history which Lt. Alexander had explained to the police, the judge and Garvey without Sky's knowledge.

Those months with Garvey had not only helped Sky avoid legal charges, they helped him get a grip on his anger and gave him a new focus.

In addition to teaching Sky to channel his anger, Garvey introduced him to a program that would encourage positive outlets which is how he got an apprenticeship to learn to do restorations.

Working with Garvey and his friends had been more valuable to getting Sky on the road to healing and letting go of some of his anger than all those sessions on that leather couch combined.

In exchange for his apprenticeship Sky would help Garvey with some of his more difficult clients. They had worked together often over the years and Sky still found it amazing that he was able to see himself in a lot of the young men that Garvey brought him in to help out with, and based on the comments made by Garvey just now on the phone this new one was going to be a doozie.

Later he would have to decide what to about his feelings, but for now all he could do was remember the day he felt his heart beat for the first time since childhood. The day he had ran into Mina buying supplies to repair a lightning strike to her barn. He could not stop himself from talking to her, from asking about her life, her horse or anything else he could think of. Really, he wanted to know everything about her.

He had asked about Zelda because he knew that was a way to get her to talk to him. He remembered how he and Josh had found her that day in waist deep mud, crying and holding on to her horse. He knew from the moment he looked into her terror-stricken eyes that he would do whatever he had to do to save that horse and her.

He had suggested that he go home with her to help, and then the next thing he knew he was waving to his sister and leaving with Mina.

He sat in the truck thinking about the first time he had seen her in the hospital and wondered how her life had been after that. Amazing that she had not changed very much since they were children.

As they were driving past the lake he realized how close he was to her and when they arrived at her place he felt more comfortable than he expected. Like he had just arrived at his home instead of hers. It had been one of those times that would mark him forever. They were unloading the supplies from the truck and just chatting about nothing when he had done the one thing he told himself he would never do, touch her. As that intense heat had passed through not just his body but his soul, he knew his life would be different; he would be different. And so he was.

The next day he had been looking for the shrubbery he wanted around the porch, when saw this Calla Lily with pink tips. It reminded him of Mina when she would blush. It warmed him all over thinking about her, so he bought the flower as a gift for her. He told himself it meant nothing but a voice in the back of his head screamed *liar* every time he tried to persuade himself to believe he felt nothing.

When he arrived at her house, she had been out so he left the flower on her step. No note, no card just the beautiful flower that reminded him of her lovely face when she smiled at him.

It never occurred to Sky that she might not know it was him. His thinking was that no one else in town ever said anything to her and she wasn't seeing anyone, so she would have to know it came from him. He walked back to his truck smiling and was sure that he had done a very nice thing for a special friend. But what he had really done was terrified a woman into feeling like the scared little girl she had been for so many years.

Chapter Five...

The Choices We Make

Lt Alexander sat in his chair staring at a photo of two children that had changed his life in more ways than anyone could imagine. He always found himself focusing on the little boy. The girl was cute and shy with her toothless little smile. All innocence and pigtails that were almost as long as she was tall, but eyes that held fear and wisdom hid behind that smile. But the little boy whose lap she sat in was different. Although his face was soft and chubby with youth the eyes that stared out at you were aged way beyond what one so young should even be familiar with. The anger and hostility held within those eyes belied years of pain, frustration and grief. Grief for the death of a childhood that happened way too soon.

He always found himself looking at the picture of Dee and Sky that had been given to him by their grandmother as a thank you for all his help. The picture had been taken quite a few years before the night he first met them. Strange how this picture gave him clarity and focus. Whenever he was faced with a difficult case and was deeply puzzled, he would take out his picture and just sit quietly and stare at it. Somehow looking at this picture reminded him of what happened when there was a loss of control and a loss of compassion and love of life. For there was no way that things like what these two beautiful children had witnessed and experienced could happen if people showed more control and compassion. If people just put self aside and loved a little more.

Meeting these two had been the beginning of his change into a different person. No one knew that he had been on the road to quickly becoming Jonathan Stephens but with a badge. Learning what they had experienced and been put through changed him almost overnight. Working the Carevelle case had nearly destroyed him and his career. For years the drinking had been his medicine but had not helped much, but the alcohol was the only way to sleep without seeing Dee & Sky's eyes and hearing that old woman's voice reciting those horrible events.

He had used alcohol, anger and a bad attitude to numb the pain he felt for what had been allowed to happen to Sky and Dee. He had known that he was on a downhill slide to disaster, but he had not been able to pull himself out of it.

His captain had even attempted to use the fact that he was a disappointment to his parents but nothing worked. Eventually he had been forced to take a leave of absence and spend some time at *Resolution* with his old military buddy Garvey and pull himself together.

But it was not to be the end of his association with that family. His second week back, he got the call to the high school where Sky had nearly beaten another student to death. He still remembered their eyes when he entered the gym that day. He also remembered the eyes of their mother when he had spoken with her. They somehow reminded him of the eyes of dead fish when he use to have time to go fishing.

Something about her eyes and her demeanor made him realize that those children had no one on their side, no one to truly care what happened to them.

It was at that time that their eyes took on a different meaning for him. When he had gone to the house to explain the details of Sky's situation to Maria Stephens he realized that he had missed so much that night long ago.

Alexander had spoken with Maria Stephens' mother out in the yard on the way back to his car and she had told him that she appreciated all that he was doing for her grandson. Sarah Jones explained that her child was not always the woman that she was now, that once Maria had been happy, loving and very talented. That her grandchildren use to be fun loving, bright precocious children getting into mischief and childlike business until their father destroyed them all in one way or another.

She had shown him the picture of her grandchildren hoping that he would look at it and remember them the way they were and not what he had come to know. The picture taken years before and given to him as a way of proving that they had been normal children. What Sarah did not know was that the only thing the picture really proved was that Jonathan Stephens really was a monster that had destroyed more than any of them realized. Bryson could hear his mother's voice reprimand him for thinking it justice that a tumor had destroyed Jonathan Stephens' brain like he had destroyed his family.

Mrs. Jones had given him the picture and he had promised himself as he drove away that he would try to remove the anger, pain and fear from their eyes if it was the last thing he ever did.

That had been the day of his last drink for breakfast, his last uncontrolled interaction with a suspect and any other behavior that could have gotten him thrown off the force.

He had a goal and a devout mission to stay in control. He had to stay on the force so that he could help those two children regain some of what had been brutally ripped away from them. He started with paying the restitution that had been ordered to prevent Sky from going to a transition center to work off the cost of Bradley Garrison's medical expenses. Then petitioning some local organizations to acquire the scholarship for DeTalia to go to college.

Introducing Sky to Garvey and having him work with Sky in his anger management program had been a brilliant and strategic move. It had won him some points with Garvey and his boss, it also gave him a way of keeping track of the Stephens' children without ever having to give anyone a reason for doing so. It was also helping him to keep the promise he made to himself to help Sky get past his anger and help Dee learn to trust.

Again, Garvey was instrumental because he knew now that Sky was helping with some of the tougher cases the he had sent Garvey's way, which in turn was helping Sky recover as well. Alexander was certain of this when he had passed by *Resolution* and saw Sky standing outside talking with a young man he had referred about four weeks before.

Now to figure out his latest problem. As always he had pulled out his photo to look into those eyes that he knew as well as he knew the pair that looked back at him from every mirror he passed. But looking at that picture did for him what it had always done, it had given him focus and purpose.

Chapter Six...

Ashley Out in the Open

Ashley lay beside the pool watching her younger daughter try to coax her older one into the pool. April was trying desperately to get Amber to join her in the water, but Amber was having none of it. She sat quietly at the edge trailing one foot in the water while she was deeply engrossed in a book that Dee had given her.

Apparently, the book was a part of a series that was all fantasy and sci-fi as the young people called it. Something called *The Phoenix Mountain Series* and Amber gobbled up those books like her little sister did cookies. She always waited anxiously for the next installment once she finished one. She had flyers, posters and T-shirts everywhere. She knew all the characters and everything about the author some *Dorsey* woman.

Ashley wished her daughter was that interested in some of the things she had tried introducing her too. Her husband had tried telling her that all young people go thru these phases and that it was nothing to concern herself with, but she felt that it was one more way that Dee was interfering in her life.

Ashley could think of no one in the world she disliked as much as her niece DeTalia. It seems she had hated the child almost from birth. The problem was the why. Well it was actually quite simple really; the child had been born to torment her and cause her nothing

29

but grief. First, she had taken her place in Maria's life. Maria had been all hers till Dee came along.

Although Dee was the second child and not the first was of no consequence. Because Sky was a boy so therefore he had been no issue at all. Then the brat came. DeTalia had come screaming into the world demanding Ashley's place in Maria's life and had gotten it without even so much as a whine. At least that was the way Ashley saw things.

For years Ashley and Maria had been a dynamic duo. They did everything together. She had even been able to sneak into her sister's room at night when she could not sleep. There were no secrets between them. Ashley even knew when Maria met boys that she liked and when she didn't.

Then there was Charles and things started to change but that was not Ashley's fault was it, she could not help that Charles had wanted her more.

Life had been hard for her when Maria left for college, but then her wonderful sister had suggested that maybe she should be allowed to come visit Maria at school for a weekend. Her mother had immediately said no, but with her sharp mind, Ashley had found a way to convince her dad that it would be a good thing for her. Eventually she was allowed to go. Oh boy what fun that had been. She got to not only visit the best sister in the whole world but be around grownups and not be treated like a baby.

Ashley very quickly learned that to keep her mother happy meant more trips to visit her sister. So that was the way it went for almost two years, then he showed up and ruined everything. Charles had been the one guy that did not pay attention to her. He made it a point to speak and smile but basically, he ignored her. How could he not have noticed how beautiful she was and that she loved him instantly.

Ashley had tried everything to get his attention and the more he ignored her the more in love with him she fell. That is until her sister ruined it. Maria had somehow figured out the way to get him to want her was to ignore him and she did it perfectly.

Ashley wanted to be with Charles so much that she was positively distracted by the fact that he seemed not to notice or to care. Ashley devised a plan to prove she was the better woman. She found out where his room was and one night went there to wait for him. When he came in and found her he had treated her like a spoiled baby and sent her back to her sister. Then he told her sister what she had done and laughed about it.

At first Maria had just insisted that she go home, then when her mother would not leave the matter be, Maria had told their mother about the incident and how embarrassed and responsible she felt for having not kept a better eye on Ashley.

How mortified Ashley had been to know that after the event that Charles found it humorous and then to know that her sister felt like she was a child that needed to be 'watched'. Ashley just knew she would die if anyone at home found out, then to arrive home and have her parents tell her that they were disappointed in her behavior.

How little did they know that their disappointment held no sway over her mortification that Charles could not see her as the woman she truly was.

The best woman for him as well, but men were stupid and gullible as her own husband had proven on a daily basis.

As if that were not bad enough when Charles shows up again in their lives what does he do, ignore her for that brat DeTalia. What could he have possibly seen in that ugly duckling of a girl. She was perfectly ready to forgive him for his stupid mistake back in college. She knew that young men often made bad choices that they would later regret and when she found out that he was spending time around Maria again she just knew that he had come back for her.

Obviously, he had not learned his lesson because what did he do, ignored her again and this time for an eleven-year-old brat that could in no way compete with her. Ashley had felt that Charles was paying so much attention to Dee just to make her jealous, which was silly really he didn't need to do that. She had been in love with him for years and was more than ready to forgive him if he had simply apologized. But what did that fool man do, go after Dee to make her jealous, as if she could be jealous of that frog of a girl.

Then Dee had the audacity to lie and say that Charles had raped her, as if. Charles was too gorgeous to need to rape anyone; all the girls wanted him especially Ashley. Oh bother, why was she sitting here wasting this beautiful day thinking about that awful woman. Truth be told, she was thinking about Dee and all the terrible things that Dee had done to her because she was at it again.

This time instead of taking the man that Ashley had wanted for herself, Dee was after the child of Ashley's very own body. Why couldn't Dee just go live on her ranch in the middle of nowhere and leave the rest of the world alone.

Ashley looked over just as April was making another attempt at getting Amber into the pool when Amber stood up and told April to stop acting like a baby, grabbed her things and started to walk away. Something about that scene made her hate Dee even more and before she got control of herself and realized what she was doing; Ashley had grabbed Amber and slapped her across the face and told her to never be that mean and call her sister a baby ever again.

The look on her husband's face was what brought her crashing back to reality. She began trying to explain her actions, but he just picked up a sobbing Amber and walked away. When Ashley turned to look at April for support, April looked at her as if she were afraid of her and turned to run behind her daddy and Amber. Ashley stood there confused and angry.

This was all Dee's fault, if she had never been born none of this would have happened. Ashley would be with Charles and Amber would love her and not Aunt Dee and April would not be looking at her like she was a monster crawled out from under the bed. Why did these terrible things keep happening to her and always as a result of the same person?

Ashley never knew it was possible to hate one person so much, but her feelings of anger for Dee had just reached a new high. She had been angry before but this latest infraction caused by Dee interfering in her life took her to a level of pisstivity that was unknown to man or woman. Something needed to be done about this heinous intrusion on her life by Dee, to teach her a valuable lesson. Ashley just needed to invent a punishment that equaled the malicious crimes committed by her niece, and she would come up with something. After all she was the better woman and that meant something.

Chapter Seven...

Amina's Nightmares Return

Amina woke up just as she had every day for the last two weeks. Crying, shaking, sweating and drenched in fear. Was it this house? Was it the flowers left at her home, was it the box of letters and pictures she had found in the attic that she spent a whole afternoon looking through. Or maybe it was him? She had never spent much time around men because they made her nervous, the only exception had been her father. That is until now. Now, there was Sky. His name was really Skylur Carrington Stephens, but that name did not fit the man that she knew. He was just Sky, and he had been with her almost every day since they had finished building the rock garden dedicated to Libby.

Amina thought back to that day that she met Sky as an adult. She had been out riding and stopped to enjoy the view of the meadow that ran along the property.

She had tied Zelda to a tree and walked a few feet away to just admire the beauty of the land.

She knew there was a lake that divided her father's property from the ranch on the other side. Amina knew there was a small Victorian house with an antebellum style at the far end of her property and that it had been bought by someone connected to the family on the other side of the lake. She had also heard about the awful things that had happened to the little girl some years back on the other side of the lake.

Something spooked Zelda and she started screaming and rearing and no matter what she did Amina could not calm her. Zelda broke her tether and ran. She was just frightened and not aware of where she was so she did not look at the ground, just ran.

By the time Amina caught sight of Zelda she had slid into a ravine filled with water from the rain and mud. Zelda tried to fight her way out, but even with all the strength from her thoroughbred parents she could not get free and try as she might Amina could not help her. She started to remember those years long ago when she had fought to get away and could not and it had frustrated her and made her curse, scream and finally cry.

That's how he found her. Muddy, angry and afraid of losing the last true love of her life. She had been barely hanging on to her horse, in waist deep mud and water with sore tired arms wrapped around Zelda's neck when he had ridden up with his beautiful little boy.

They had asked no questions, promised nothing but delivered her and her precious Zelda safely to dry land. Amina looked at him briefly, thank him and rode off on her tired and weak horse.

She had spent many weeks thinking about the man that had helped her with her horse. She thought about his eyes and how they had not changed much over the years. She thought about how he had looked the first time she saw him and how he had watched her with those eyes. Eyes that seem to speak of their own accord. Eyes that told a tale of a horrible childhood and innocence gone way too soon. Eyes that seem to convey a message much like the one that her own eyes told. But Amina also remembered that he had saved her that day, the same way he had saved her all those years ago.

Mina walked over and stared out the window at the fence, the fence that Sky had helped her repair. She remembered that he had come to the ranch under the guise of checking on her horse and helping repair the fence, maybe even to check on her.

She had been stacking boards on the truck to repair damage to the fence around the property. Strange, that she could never think of this place as home. Home meant comfort, peace and safety, things that she felt she may never experience again as long as he lived. But then she had run into Sky and everything began to change, even Sky.

He had asked what she was about with the boards and boxes of nails. She told him that there had been repairs that needed to be done and she was headed out to complete them. He offered to help her, not sure why, she said yes.

They had worked on the fence till dusk fell and then sat on the crest of the hillside and watched the sun set. No conversation, just quiet companionship and a sense of comfort she had not experienced with any other man except her father. Then he started talking to her about what he did to keep his hands and mind occupied. Something he had learned after life had taken him down some dark roads. How he had met two men that taught him all people were not the same. That there are some people that when you met them, you get a feeling that they are different and that sometimes you have to let down your guard and just trust because your heart tells you too.

Amina and Sky had run into each other two weeks ago in the store and he asked about her horse. She really liked his shyness. She felt at ease with him in a way she never had with anyone. They had talked about Zelda and he told her about restoring an old antebellum style house at the far end of his sister's property. She looked into his eyes and saw the truth, that he chose that house because it kept him near his sister and maybe near her.

Mina, for reasons she could not explain, told him that lightning had hit the barn where she kept her horse supplies and she was going home to repair the damage before the coming rain. Sky had walked her out to her truck and asked if he could catch a ride with her. Again, uncertain why she had agreed, she told him yes and watched as he waved bye to his sister and climbed in the truck cab beside her.

He rode home with her and they talked, but she could not remember about what.

Once they reached her property she started to unload the truck and he touched her hand and told her no. She could still feel the bolt of energy that ran up her arm, exploded in her chest and flowed down to her toes. She knew he felt it too because he immediately removed his hand and began unloading the truck.

It was the day after her soul stirring experience with Sky that she had come home late and found it. The portent of evil sitting there looking as beautiful as it was dangerous. Sure no one would believe her if she told them that white Calla Lilies with pink tips were dangerous. Most women loved them and always thought they were special if they received them because they were expensive and hard to grow. Not Mina.

Mina hated them because they were *his* flower. The one '*he*' chose because he said it reminded him of her when her cheeks were all pink from blushing, which she always did as a child because she was so shy. Jeremiah had started giving her the pretty flower that she learned to hate about two months before all hell broke loose. It was also his calling card. A way that he would let her know that he had been to her room looking for her and she had not been there. He would leave one on her pillow.

After her father had taken her away from her mom, Jeremiah would have the flowers sent to her or left on her step so that she would know that he had found her or been looking for her and she had not been there.

Once her father had found the flower and asked her about it, because he had thought it was from some boy at school, until Mina had told George the truth about the flower. They had moved that same evening.

That was the way it had been till Jeremiah had been sent to prison again. Of course, he always got out and came looking for her.

Her father always moved them around and not settled anywhere too long. George was always looking for the next place to move his daughter to keep her out of Jeremiah's reach.

Mina thought she was ok and had a little more time till she had come home a few weeks ago and found that evil calling card on her step. Why now? Why the day after she and Sky had really connected. The day he had touched her hand and she felt every nerve in her body light up like the 4th of July.

It was scary but wonderful because she knew that he had felt it too. They had seen each other every day since then and she still did not have the nerve to tell him she really was here because she was hiding from someone.

A week ago they had run into each other in town and she told him that if he was not careful she would think that he was following her.

He told her that people were going to think that they were planning their trips to town just to pretend to run into each other. They had both laughed about it but, Mina had no idea why that had been so funny.

But she did remember a strange sensation that came over her but before she could focus on it, Sky asked her to give him a ride to his truck at the other end of the street.

Again he had ended up coming home with her and they had sat talking till the wee hours of the morning. Mina asked him if he still wrote poetry and he told her no, that he had stopped in his teen years because it was too much of a reminder.

She had wanted to ask, a reminder of what but thought better of it because when you ask for a revelation that somehow required you to render one of your own.

The only revelation that she felt would satisfy one of that caliber would be to tell him about the monster that not only chased her in her dreams.

The one reason she never wanted to tell Sky the truth was because she knew he would try to help, protect her somehow and she did not want him hurt because '*he*' was free and he was looking for her, so she very well may have to leave this place.

Jeremiah always kept his word and he always did as he said he would do. Her last memory was of him yelling that she belonged to him and he never gave up what was his. That memory and those words were what kept her awake at night. What drove her from her own dreams and what had owned her dreams since she was ten years old. Why that Lily on her step meant nothing good would last for her and why she really needed to leave.

When Mina's father had gained custody of her he never wanted her near her mother or anything that would remind her of that time. But once the truth about Jeremiah had come out, it was explained to Mina. Her father never wanted her to know but he was overruled by the therapist and Mina was told everything.

All the truth did for Mina was become fuel for nightmares where Jeremiah carried out his threat and her father could not save her. So every time the fear returned so did the nightmares, Mina wondered would she ever be free, would she ever be safe.

First the flower, then the feeling had grown in intensity a week ago when she had felt someone watching her and Sky as they talked beside her truck the day they had laughed about always running into each other in town and people thinking it was planned by one or the other of them. She had disregarded her feelings as paranoia groomed from so many years avoiding being found by her stepfather, but she could not ignore that tight feeling at the base of her neck and that itch in the center of her spine like someone was drilling a hole in her with their eyes.

Chapter Eight...

Evil Has a Handsome Face

Jeremiah had considered it fate when he had run into the young lady that had been a young Mina's neighbor at the gas station. Although, his initial reaction had been concerning that he may have to do something "unkind" to her when she first spoke his name across the parking lot. But his good fortune held when he realized that she had been away at a girls' school and had not heard about all those things that had been spread thru town about him. Yes, luckily this cute little pixie of a girl had gone off to a girl's school and been stupid enough to enjoy it.

At least that was Jeremiah's way of thinking. No sensible girl would enjoy being sent away, and he had actually surprised himself by asking her about it.

It was then that he found out that her father had been one of the local ministers at the church and only by going away to school had she been allowed to experience any of the things young girls consider to be fun.

Jeremiah found himself imagining what it might be like to have spent some time with her as a young girl and properly introduced her to womanhood and not have her learn with some fumbling idiot of a boy, probably in the backseat of his parent's car. Then he found himself wondering if teenagers still did that sort of thing. He caught himself reaching toward the girl and had to pretend to be opening her car door to cover the unexpected motion.

She had provided him with some useful information in the midst of her simpleminded chatter. She told him that she had heard that Mina and her dad had planned to move to a place where they could raise horses. He should have known, Mina had always had a fondness for those filthy animals. He had developed an intense hatred for horses when he had been bitten and kicked by the same horse on multiple occasions. He had been told it was his fault for mistreating the animal, but he had never accepted that reasoning because after all it was just an animal.

Figures that Mina's father would be a horse lover, would explain why she did and why he had eventually allowed her mother to hang some pictures in her room and bought her a stuffed pony to gain her trust.

Jeremiah had been fortunate enough to uncover the last three places that George had taken his Mina to live. All nasty, despicable places to have taken his precious girl. But all this searching and uncovering had accomplished was confirmation that he was better for Mina than her own father. Of course there were many that would find fault with his reasoning, especially the penal system that he had escaped from, the families of the correctional officers that he had murdered during his escape and the members of the parole board that said he was a danger to society, which had been their reason for not releasing him.

During Jeremiah's search of the beach condo he had discovered, he found several partially burned bills in the fireplace that gave him the idea to come back to this ugly little town where he had been unwise enough to move with his own daughter all those years ago. Once he arrived he wondered if he would be able to learn anything useful.

These people had never liked nor trusted him so it was doubtful he would find someone to talk to him. More likely he would find himself staring down the barrel of a gun of some police officers that wanted to play hero because some good citizen had alerted them to his presence.

But as he had paid for his gas at the pump, the safest way if he did not wish to be seen by a clerk that possibly knew his face, the very thing he attempted to avoid happened. "Mr. Senior, is that you?" Jeremiah had turned expecting to see someone he would have to hurt, but instead he saw the grown-up version of the skinny little girl with braces that had been Mina's playmate at one time. She told him that she remembered him because he had reminded her of the dreamy guy in one of her favorite movies. That had made Jeremiah smile and she began to smile and bat her lashes like silly women did to get a man's attention.

Strangely enough the type of females that attracted his attention never did that but little girls did not know how to be coy, just shy which was what he really liked the most about them.

She told him a whole lot of things that did not interest him about her life and college and being single and her father dying in an accident.

He was not sure what she was really going on about, until she mentioned something about Mina passing thru town and heading to her lake house with a horse trailer. He then began to pay close attention to her conversation, she only needed a little prodding to tell him what she knew. It was not much but he had found Mina before with much less to go on.

After she had given him all the information that he considered valuable, he wanted to get in his stolen vehicle and leave, but he had to keep her from getting suspicious about his questions or his appearance in town especially if she ran into someone that felt the need to tell her about his past indiscretions.

His intense desire to get away from this annoying pest of a female, disturbed his focus in such a way that he caught himself about do something that would certainly cause unwanted attention. So he covered his mistake with the gentlemanly gesture of opening her car door. Once she was inside and engaging her seatbelt he made his exit.

Driving through this town was not a smart idea but he had wasted enough time and this was the shortest route to where he needed to go next, the bills in the fireplace had been for supplies and had an address that he had mistaken for the place where they had been shipped from but now he knew it was where they were shipped to. The place where he would find his Mina.

When he arrived he had found a hidden little corner of the earth that the world never knew existed. After having been there for three weeks he had learned nothing to indicate that Mina was here or ever had been and was thinking it was time to leave when he saw the local sheriff looking at the license plate of his fourth stolen vehicle.

He had changed the plates but felt that close inspection of the vehicle would reveal the broken steering column, so of course it was time to move on.

Sitting in the car perusing a map contemplating his next destination, a sound from his past floated gently to his ears. He almost thought it was an hallucinations until the breeze brought the sound softly to him again and he looked up to see Mina laughing and talking with a young man that was looking at her with intense ownership in his eyes.

Jeremiah reached for both the door handle and his hunting knife before he realized his own movements. He regained control of himself and just sat there caressing the blade until he noticed the sharp sting in the tip of his thumb and looked down to see that he had sliced open his own finger. Mina had always had a way of unsettling him and disturbing his concentration, it was a bittersweet pleasure to know nothing had changed.

Finally, lady luck was beginning to play nice with him. He had found her, after all these long weeks of searching he had found his muse, the motivation for his life to continue and reason so many others life had ended. He followed Mina's truck as long as he dared. He did not need to follow her home because the man with her looked wary of everything and everyone and he had no desire to be noticed. Not yet and not by anyone but Mina. Time to plan and prepare.

Chapter Nine...

The Bane of Erica's Existence

E rica walked into her beautiful glass building thinking that
had life made a few less subtle turns she would be a different
woman with a whole other life. She rode the elevator up to her
condo thinking about a glass of the nice '65 Bordeaux she had along
with a long hot bath. She could almost taste the smooth wine and
feel the deep calm that eased over her as the wine flowed thru her
and the warm heat enveloped her body. But when the elevator doors
opened, and she saw the reflection of the woman primping herself in
the full-length mirror, all thoughts of wine and comfort left her. Of
all the things she was not interested in doing tonight, talking to her
mother had to be at the top of the list. Just seeing the woman seemed
to sap her happy thoughts.

"Hello Erica," even the way her name rolled off the woman's
tongue made her feel bad. Her mother had a way of looking at her
that made her feel like a complete failure, like everything wrong in
the world could be laid at her feet.

Everything from her father's sudden heart attack to the terrorist
attacks of 9/11 were possibly somehow linked to Erica's existence on
earth. Although she was never sure why, Erica knew that her mother
blamed her for AJ's defection, her mother's word not hers, because
surely he would not have chosen Leslie Smith over her if Erica had
not contributed to it in some way.

Elyssa Cason-Grant stood looking at the daughter that she had never understood, never really knew. Elyssa was raised to believe that children, especially daughters were simply tools to be used to accomplish one's goals in life. They did not require anything more than to be taught refined manners and behavior, that they were to be indulged and spoiled only enough to give them a taste of the finer things in life. The goal was to solidify the drive that was placed in them to always succeed. So where had she gone wrong with Erica.

Erica had been groomed from infancy to be the perfect tool. Erica had been sent to all the right schools, attended all the right events and functions, she even had the additional gift of her father's intelligence; but none of it could withstand the tidal wave of feelings that she had failed miserably to keep in check for Giovanni Smith, III. Really, where had she gone wrong.

From the moment she had met AJ, Erica knew she was doomed. He was every woman's fantasy and a whole lot more. The first mistake Erica had made was telling her mother about AJ. After her first visit to his parent's house she had come home excited.

She went straight to her room to spend some quiet time with her diary. The one place she could speak her mind without being placed on the platform of scrutiny, where she could say whatever she wanted and there would be no long looks of disappointment.

While writing in her diary, Erica did not have to be perfect and proper every single moment or risk one of her mothers' looks of anger. No fear of embarrassing herself or saying something that would make people think she had been raised by a herd of cows. Just one of the many ways her mother used to describe Erica's behavior or appearance or her body.

Erica had not been able to contain her excitement at having met AJ and having been talked to as a young lady and not as her mother's greatest disappointment. She was busy writing and so deeply involved that she did not notice her mother entering her room. This visit was no different from many others. Her mother would enter her room and find her lying on her bed on her belly with her feet in the air without socks or shoes and chewing on a number two pencil, deep in thought.

Erica could still hear her mother's voice in her head just as clear and irritating then as it was now. "Erica dear, refined young ladies do not chew on pencils." This was said as she took Erica's last sharpened pencil and threw it in the trash. "Ladies of breeding and class do not dawdle around with their feet bare swaying in the breeze." As she not so gently pushed Erica's feet down and turned her around to pull her up to a sitting position. This scene played out all through Erica's adolescent years until she left for that hellish place in Geneva called Lafayette School for Girls. It was really a four-story torture chamber run by 16 women that hated everyone including themselves.

Elyssa had asked Erica what had her so engrossed that she could ignore her own mother, Erica responded that she had gone out with her daddy and met some very interesting people. Of course before she could complete any sentence, something she said was corrected by her mother. This time it was 'father' instead 'daddy'. Erica never saw Taylor Mackenzie Cason as a father, he was and would always be daddy. But her mother never liked the familiar term and said it was something people with no class or dignity called their fathers. Erica never agreed but had learned after two or three solid backhands from her mother not to disagree, but simply allow her mother to think she had won and just continue on, until the next correction which was never long in coming.

Erica told her mother that she was invited back and her mother said that she did not approve of Erica traipsing behind her father like a pet dog and that she should be doing more important things like studying her French and Italian so that she could speak fluently instead of brutalizing her mother's favorite languages as if she were raised in a barn by horses and pigs.

When Erica finally finished her telling of the day's events with her mother's constant corrections, she noticed that her mother was not really listening but staring out the window. After a few minutes of silence her mother turned to her and said that she thought Erica needed to exercise more and spend less time dawdling and scratching in that journal.

Elyssa often said that Erica's writing had no flare or grace. Erica looked down at her handwriting and remembered that her mother had said that her handwriting was the equivalent of chickens stepping in ink and scratching on paper.

Were it not for her daddy Erica's childhood would have been a complete horror. Her father always hugged her and kissed the freckle at the tip of her nose where he swore an angel had kissed her at birth.

He would lift her up on his shoulders and ride her through the house, or swing her around until they both were dizzy and falling on the floor laughing hysterically. That was her favorite part because she loved to see her daddy smile and to hear him laugh out loud.

That was really the problem wasn't it. Erica found out around her ninth birthday that her parents did not like each other and it was a shock. Her mother had been insistent on marrying a man with wealth and power that would cater to her and give her all the things her parents had not. Erica's father wanted a wife that would play tennis and give him children.

Neither got what they wanted and so they tolerated each other and pretended to ignore that which bothered them the most about each other, everything.

Her daddy would not indulge or tolerate her mother's excessive shopping for things that were not necessary; so her mother refused to have more than one child and stopped attempting to play tennis. She never liked it, and was not very good and even with lessons was not a suitable doubles partner. So, she simply wore the appropriate attire and went to the club and left the actual playing to her husband

and those brutish females that were the equivalent of brood mares that grunted and sweated like farm animals.

That was her childhood until Lafayette. All these memories cascaded through her mind as she opened the door and entered her condo with her mother behind her staring at her home like she was afraid something would mar the Chanel suit she wore.

Chapter Ten...

More Than Words

As her mother began speaking about something Erica knew for sure would not matter in the least to her, she continued her perusal through a segment of memories that always arrived unbidden just like her mother. Her mother mentioned her father's name and it caught her attention for a few brief clicks of time. It was something that still gave her pause. All her life Erica's father had been known as Cason. No one, not even her mother called her father anything but Cason. Occasionally, but only in public, her mother would call him 'dear', a word that Erica had learned to hate as much as the word 'father'.

Erica had learned not to use 'daddy' around her mother because it angered her. Erica now knew it was anger driven by jealousy of the close relationship between her and her father.

But to Erica he would always be daddy and Erica loved and lived for father's smiles; and would do almost anything to have one bestowed upon her.

Her father's smiles were everything to her. They were her 'thank yous', her praise for a deed well done, her trophies and all that made her feel loved. This was especially true after about the age of twelve, when she ceased to be able to please her mother in any way, shape form or fashion. Because she could not do anything well according to her mother, she did not receive praise from her mother or a feeling of being wanted or loved.

Most young ladies got the stand up straight, hold your head up, or the smile more tirade from their mothers; Elyssa Cason was cut from a different bolt of cloth, so Erica got the constant criticism and verbal assaults that was meant to act as motivation. When that did not work, her mother was not above a solid backhand to the mouth or face. None of these did anything to endear her to her daughter, if anything they made her learn to distance herself and cling to her daddy and love him with all her adolescent heart. That is until AJ nudged him aside and then she really felt the sting of her mother's barbed tongue. Once Elyssa learned about his family and his pedigree all her focus became marrying him to her daughter.

Elyssa stood staring at the woman that had brought her nothing but grief from conception till now. As Erica poured a glass of the wine that she had suddenly reacquired a desire for, her mother watched and began to wonder for the millionth time if maybe her real daughter had been switched at birth and that would explain so much about the failure that stood disheveled and haggard before her.

A mistake that would explain why this woman had none of her grace, class and dignity. Why she insisted on being around her father instead of clinging to the invaluable lessons attempted by her mother.

Elyssa could not fathom how Erica could have lost her wits and thrown away the golden opportunity to have the most perfect man in the world. That is, until Elyssa met Richard Delvin Grant. He was the man of her dreams and the man that her mother had groomed her for and she had wasted no time ensuring that he knew it.

They were married after a six-month courtship, with no prenup but unlike Cason, there was no tennis, and no desire for children. Her life was finally perfect, until Delvin suggested that he meet her daughter. Why did men always have to prove that they were not perfect after all.

Erica just wanted Elyssa to state her business and leave, there was another glass of wine and a bottle of Jasmine bubble bath in her immediate future and like always Elyssa was in the way.

Erica vaguely remembered that Elyssa had remarried and that he was powerful and wealthy all the things that mattered to her and that Erica could care less about.

"So why are you here," Erica had thought it but her mouth heard it and decided to echo the words out loud. Elyssa gave her one of the looks that screamed you are such a disappointment. Instead of shrinking inside herself as she had always done, Erica stepped out of her 4 inch heels and walked barefoot across the room and sat with one foot tucked under her and running the toes of her other foot across the carpet.

Elyssa glanced at the deep red polish on her daughter's toes and gave an involuntary wrinkling of her nose. Elyssa felt that ladies did not go barefoot and therefore had absolutely no reason to paint their toes. "Really dear, must you saunter around with your feet uncovered?"

"My home, my feet, my rules." Erica stated in the nastiest tone of voice she could. "Again, why are you here?"

Elyssa took a calming breath because she knew that Erica was going to make this much more difficult than was necessary. "Delvin wants to meet you and introduce you to some people of significance that can further your career." Elyssa said this with a facial expression that was suggestive of someone that had eaten something, then discovered it was not what they thought it was.

Elyssa, said ladies of refinement did not work except to improve the prestige of their husbands.

Before Elyssa could continue her monologue of the benefits of Erica doing what she wanted, Erica got up from her seat walked to the door, opened it and said, "get out." "I do not give one wit of a damn about your husband and his collection of snobs. All I want is for you to leave and never come back. Because unlike you, I loved my daddy and still miss him dearly. I have no interest in you or helping you put on a charade for Delvin or anyone else. I still have the echo of all the evil things you said to me the day I lost my daddy so do us both a favor and leave before I completely forget the biological ties between us and act like the animal you have compared me to all my life."

Elyssa walked out without another word and headed for the elevator. As the doors closed she dropped her chin to her chest and let go of the breath that she had been holding as well as the tears that she had refused to cry.

How could one person hold so much hostility and anger. But the truth was Elyssa knew how, the way she had been taught all her life. The grief and self-hate she had been carrying since her husband's death broke free of the chains and erupted from her in tidal waves.

She swore she would never treat her child as she had been treated, but as she stood there looking at her reflection, she knew that she had become the worst of all evils; her own mother and the realization made the tears flow faster.

Chapter Eleven...

Never Any Real Answers

Charles realized the only way to stop this was to tell Maria the truth, not the court version but the real truth. But what would come of that, not only did he not know he no longer cared.

Charles stood and looked out the tiny little window and wondered what the world had become now that he was no longer a part of it. Strangely he did not miss his freedom until he found out that Libby had passed and he had not been able to see her or say goodbye, or even offer his last respects.

How could one woman have become so important to him and how could he have disappointed her so. Even after he promised he would behave over and over, Libby always knew him better than he knew himself and would tell him that he would do better next time with God's help. Maybe that's why he never got better because he never really asked for God's help. Libby always said that God won't force His way into your life, you have to ask Him and Charles had never gotten around to the asking part.

Charles turned and faced the woman he had known for most of his adult life and tried to figure out where to start. He guessed now would be as good a time as any to ask God's help, because surely he needed it.

Charles began by telling Maria that he was sorry for all that had happened, for everything that he had done. He did not offer excuses for there were none. He told her that Libby had been right that he needed help and should have gotten it long ago. The why, was another matter. He told Maria that he had always liked and been attracted to women that were small and petite. The more childlike the more intense his attraction. Which was why he was initially drawn to her. By the end of their first year in college he knew she would never tolerate him and his foolishness as Libby would call it. But just kept her as friend and let his mind tell him that he was better, but his heart had always whispered to him at night that not only was he a pedophile he was a liar as well.

He told her the truth came out when he met her sister Ashley. Ashley was all the things he had loved about young girls and he knew if he did not keep his distance that he would be in trouble, again.

Maria looked up at Charles and the unasked question hung there like a large purple elephant standing in the room.

While there was to be truth telling, Charles knew he may as well let all the cats out the bag. Before he had even decided for certain to tell Maria the truth, his mouth had made a decision and started talking. He began telling Maria about his first realization that he was different and that he had a problem. It had started when had met his first real friend in high school. They had clicked immediately gotten along great. Played sports together, hung out and rode around together as Charles had a car and his buddy did not. Life was great, he had real friends and people that had his back and he mattered too. Problem was, he was not a real friend and the guy did not matter as much to him. He had gone to the guy's house often and had seen his little sister, but she never paid him any mind so it was easy to ignore her.

That is until his senior year and she was about to be 13 years old. He went to her birthday party thinking it was a kiddie party and he would be bored to death.

He arrived with a *Barnes and Noble* gift card because she loved to read and he had no idea what else to give her.

He walked out on the deck and got sucker punched, this was a pool party and there was a whole slew of 13 and 14-year-old girls and his eyes almost started to bleed from all the little girl flesh being exposed. He had to keep drinking punch to keep his tongue from hanging out like a dog in summer heat without water.

Somehow his buddy forgot to mention the pool part when he told him to come over for his kid sister's party. Charles tried turning his back to the pool and just pretended to watch the game on the television that some of the adults were watching. This worked until the guy's sister came to say thanks for the gift card and that it was an awesome gift. Then the real test happened when she wanted to hug him to say thanks. He failed miserably and he knew it, he just hoped no one else knew.

He stayed for another 15 minutes and when he could not keep his eyes from wandering towards the pool or keep the activity going on in his shorts from becoming obvious he pretended he needed to be somewhere else and left.

He avoided his buddy for two weeks and then he made the mistake of dropping by to catch up and no one was home but the guy's little sister. She insisted that he come in and wait for her brother who would be back in half an hour.

Every cell in his brain screamed at him to just leave and come back later, but Charles needed to prove he was stronger than his urges. Again, he failed.

Sitting there trying not to look at the girl, all long legs and arms, two pigtails and glasses were making him sweat. Then she started talking to him and smiling and giggling because she thought he was really cute.

So many mistakes made but none worse than letting her show him her tattoo that she had gotten for her birthday that her parents did not know about. It was high on her hip and was a cute little rosebud with a butterfly.

Charles had never seen anything more sexy and inviting in his whole life and he knew when he told her he thought she was cute and she asked him if he really thought so, that he was in deep kimchi.

One moment they were sitting across from each other and he was trying to keep his eyes on the floor and the next she was in his lap, kissing him and his hands were in places that he had fantasized about since her party. She let him do whatever he wanted and touch whatever he could get to without undressing her. The old gym shorts made his explorations easy and oh so satisfying.

Maria sat there stunned and speechless, she could not believe that he was admitting to having taken advantage of a 13-year-old girl when he was 18. The part that made her search frantically for the trash can because she was about to lose that cheeseburger, was that sitting there looking at him Maria could tell that not only did he enjoy what had happened between him and that poor girl, he was excited by the memory of it as well.

Charles told her that he came to his senses as he was about to go for the button on his jeans and she started trying to help him. Charles said he stood up and told her he needed to go. He ran out the door and drove away with his tires screeching. He thought he passed his buddy walking back to his house but did not stop or look too closely for confirmation. There was no way he could stop and talk to the guy with the taste and the smell of the guy's little sister all over him.

He went home, locked himself in his room and stayed in his shower for about two hours doing what he had been doing every night since the pool party.

He fully expected the cops to show up at his house or at school and did not go back for about three days. When nothing happened but the guy kept calling to ask if everything was ok and to invite him to hang out, Charles figured that the girl never told anyone what had happened.

He went to school but avoided the guy at school and never went back to the house, and never interacted with any of the other guys at school he occasionally talked to and remained antisocial the last four weeks of school. He graduated and moved away. Maria sat there staring blankly blinking like an owl. She could not get her mouth to work or her tongue to unglue itself from the roof of her mouth, like it did not want any part of that conversation.

Charles took her silence as encouragement to continue, so he told her that a few more similar events had occurred between that experience and having met her and her sister Ashley.

Charles explained that he had never gone beyond touching and kissing until he met Dee. He said that none of the others had that true innocence that he wanted till he met DeTalia. Maria spoke, but he was so deep in his reverie that he was beyond hearing her tell him not to speak her daughter's name that way.

Charles said he was not certain what had initially kept him in control, but he knew he was done when he found himself noticing and constantly watching how shy and young Dee was. That she never really knew what was coming or what to expect until it was already happening and by then he had gone too far to even stop himself.

Marie was out of the chair screaming, clawing and hitting Charles before the guards could get into the room and pull her off him.

All she could do was scream at him as they held her arms and drug her from the visitation room. His last thought was that he was on the floor bleeding again.

Strangely enough, he was becoming familiar with that experience as he had been beaten and attacked so many times that first year in prison that he had come to expect the violence and knew that would have been his way of life for the remainder of his prison sentence, that is if he had not been placed in Protective Custody after the last attack.

The guards had not cared if he died by natural causes or was murdered by the other inmates, either way their thinking was that his death would have been justified. But unfortunately for the guards and the other inmates, the group that owned and operated the prison did not want his death because his presence brought interest and therefore funding to the facility. He was put in permanent *PC;* his guards were rotated daily and were chosen by lottery drawing during shift change so no one ever really knew who would be guarding him.

Of course, Maria was escorted out and told she was banned from visiting again, as if she would really come back to see that animal. How she wished she had left the questions unanswered, her ignorance intact and just gone on with her life as her daughter had done. Maria sat in her car with her head resting on the steering wheel still shaking, still so very angry.

If ever there was a time she needed to see a therapist, this was it. Maria berated herself for thinking that she had needed to see Charles, that she had had to speak to him in person. But just as in times before, her mother, her husband and her therapist had tried to discourage her from visiting him, but like always she would not listen to anyone but her own mind. Look where that had gotten her, headed back to the therapy couch.

Chapter Twelve...

Bradley's Emotional Restitution

Because Bradley was never sure what about that day drove his actions, he had chosen to blame Sky all these years. Now sitting here in a court appointed anger management session he was forced to really evaluate himself and his actions.

Bradley had begun seeing the truth after about his 4th session. Sessions nine and ten had made it painfully obvious that he could no longer project the blame on anyone but himself. Here well into his 7th week, about the 13th session, the truth was like a drunk on a street corner with a bull horn. He was angrier about having been beaten, than the source of the beating. After years of having his ego stroked by his overindulging mother and being constantly under compensated or acknowledged by the football coach and team that he had given so much too; Bradley was just angry to find himself in a place he had never been, except occasionally on the football field.

Now where to go from here. For starters he would complete all twenty-four of his court ordered sessions. Yes, every one of the twice a week for twelve weeks sessions. Then he could be sure that he was on the right road. Part of his healing that would include learning how to help others deal with their anger and other dangerous emotions in a way that would not leave behind a long list of emergency room visits and unnecessary injuries that could be avoided as well as a laundry list of problems and hurt people that were trying to bear the weight of guilt for someone they loved or cared for. It's amazing what four broken ribs and a metal plated jaw could do for accomplishing an attitude adjustment. Saying that pain was an intervention was not just an understatement, but a true eye opener. That play on words made Bradley smile to himself.

Bradley did not give much thought to all the other injuries, fights, arrests and nights in a holding cell. It was just that initial fight that dominated his thoughts and affected his reasoning. Amazing how all those weeks in a wheelchair intended to alleviate pain and stress did nothing but realign his thought processes and that six months of drinking through a straw increased his desire for self-control.

Bradley knew the road to atonement was not paved but rocky and filled with potholes requiring much patience and dedication to fill in the damage done by all his years of stupidity.

But very little in this world meant as much to him as his sister and his new-found dignity. He knew he was about to enter into a 12-round fight that only God could help him win. But prayer and faith were things that he had been learning more and more about and those along with Garvey's help would surely bring him out of this the victor.

As Bradley sat waiting for his session leader to finish speaking with the other participants, an idea began taking shape. A plan to remove him from the negative place he had kicked in the door to enter as well as an olive branch for Melody. His sister had made it clear in no uncertain terms that she had made her last trip to the hospital or police station for what she called tomfoolery.

Amazing too, how the loss of love and support from one's family will do much for awakening one from a coma of idiocracy. That day Melody had left him in his apartment in his wheelchair, had a totally different feeling now. Then it was just hurt feelings because Mel would not be around to coddle, pet him and continually refill his cup of self-pity.

Now her absence was motivation and encouragement to make the life altering changes that her pleas and tears had not all those years before.

Garvey was the only name the group had been given for the large man with the missing left hand that lead the anger management sessions at *Resolutions*, but Bradley had long since stopped caring about who he was and how he had lost his hand. But focused solely on his ability to help them all accomplish their mission. As Mr. Garvey approached, Bradley attempted to mentally pose the questions he would ask and what he planned to do with the answers he received.

Surprisingly, Bradley left an hour later with more excitement than he had experienced in more than five years. Life was changing. In about two weeks he would be off his crutches and able to walk maybe just with a cane. Then Mr. Garvey would introduce him to a young man that would hopefully change his life. Little did Bradley know that this man had already changed his life once before, many years ago at a high school dance.

Chapter Thirteen...

What Would Libby Say

"My mother hates me." Although that is not how the conversation started, that is the part that registered in Dee's mind as the beginning. All she could do was ask the obvious question, and Amber told her that her mother had yelled at her and when Dee attempted to explain that sometimes people did things that they did not intend to do; that was when she had been thrown back into the middle of her horrific past by Amber telling her that Ashley had slapped and shook her. She had gotten up and started moving before Vanni could get an answer as to her destination in her underwear in the middle of the night.

Her mind no longer registered, nor honestly remembered how the conversation started, but she knew it had left her shaken and she could not get control of herself and as always Vanni had to referee the match between Dee and her emotions.

She was actually downstairs putting on a sweater and grabbing her keys, before Vanni finally convinced her to stop, look down at herself and see that she was practically naked. It was then that he got an answer about what had been said to her over the phone and by who.

The call had come more than two weeks ago, but the sound of her voice still rang fresh in Dee's ears. The call had left her angry and shaken, Vanni had spent half the night trying to talk her out of going to Ashley's house to get Amber; then the rest of the night talking her out of the horrific scenarios she was creating in her head about what was happening to the girl.

As Dee got dressed for the day she could not help thinking back to the phone call she had received from her young cousin Amber. She had not been able to completely excise the sound of the child's voice from her head. Every quiet moment since the call had been short lived as the reverie continued to replay in her head and behind her lids if ever her eyes were closed when the memory stormed into her thoughts.

Dee thought about it differently now, but she still thought that she should have gone to pick up Amber or maybe talk to her at least, but she doubted that Ashley would have let her near Amber or have allowed Amber to leave the house.

Ashley seemed to act as if the things in her life that had gone wrong were all Dees' fault. Dee could not imagine what she could have done to make her aunt act the way she did. Dee thought about some of the things that Ashley had said both to her and about her over the years and she tried to think of something that she could have done to provoke Ashley to such a passionate dislike for her. Always Dee came up with nothing. But something in her mind told her that Ashley would give a different answer if asked.

This was one of those times when having Libby around would have made life so much better. Libby would tell her what to do and how to move forward. But of course that was not possible. She would never be able to ask Libby's advice again. But there was a second best option. Libby had once told her that, *"people can't save you, so don't let them break you."* Libby explained that people did not have the power to save lives as Christ had when he died on the cross for our sins, so we should not allow them to take power and control over our lives with their hate and meanness.

As she sat there hearing Libby's voice recite those words she remembered what Libby had told her at her passing, that she was leaving her in good hands. Not just God's but Dee assumed Vanni's as well.

But the truth of the matter is that through Vanni God had blessed her with another woman that she loved and respected and that would talk to her and help her with anything.

Dee thought about what she would say as she headed to the den to call Bella, she would be able to offer her some way of dealing with her feelings if not her aunt.

Tatianna Smith answered the phone on the second ring. Tia, as her husband called her, felt that if someone thought enough of you to call you, then you should appreciate them enough to answer.

Dee asked Tia, Bella as she called her, all the questions that she would have loved to ask Libby. Of course Tia answered with all the love and reassurance that Libby would have given but it had a different flavor to it, because Libby was gone.

Dee had to remind herself to listen to the conversation in her ear and not the one in her head. As with every conversation that she had with Bella, Dee found herself thinking about how much talking to her was like talking with Libby. The same wise words, the same bible references that made Dee think hard, the same strategic pauses to give the information time to sink in. Bella was honest with Dee in a way that made her feel like she was talking with Libby, instead of a woman she had only known for a few short years.

Dee had never been made to feel tolerated or as just a daughter-in-law, she felt truly apart of this woman and was always reminded how special she was to all of them and how very blessed Bella and Papa were to have her and all the love she and the children had brought to Vanni and their entire family.

Love that she had not known existed till she met Libby and then Vanni. She had a desire now to share that love with everyone, her brother, her mother, her nieces and especially her aunt.

As Dee sat musing about the comfort of being loved, appreciated and welcomed; another of her favorite people walked in the room, Angel. Angel helped her and Vanni around the ranch, kept the children calm and cooked a mean casserole. Although, she had amnesia and no memory of the life she had before her accident; she loved the ranch and all the people there like family. And to them she was family. Dee knew one-day Angel's memory would return and she would be gone as quick as she came, but until that day came Angel was like the sister she never had and didn't realize she missed until now.

Dee made a mental note to ask Monty about working with Angel to try to recover something that may help her remember, especially since Dee knew that was one of the reasons Angel was the way she was. She did not know who or what she was before, and it drove her to frustration at times trying to force the memories to return.

Chapter Fourteen...

Let Sleeping Dogs Lie

Sky never knew why walking helped him to think more clearly, why when he walked along aimlessly he could focus and create some of the most interesting ideas. He could work out some of the most difficult details of a restoration project just by walking around, going nowhere and headed in no particular direction.

Just as he was about to turn and head back to his original destination, which was his favorite restaurant for dinner, something caught his attention as he was about to head in the door. He saw a familiar reflection in the glass. He turned and saw someone he had not seen in years but had to rethink all his feeling about seeing now. Sky stood there looking at Ricardo and wondering where he had been and what he had been doing all these years.

As Sky watched Ric, he missed the dark sports car across the street with the driver watching him. Jeremiah watched Sky trying to see if he could figure out what it was that Mina saw when she looked at him.

Ricardo felt himself being watched and looked up into Sky's face and wondered the same things that Sky had just been thinking about him. Ric did not smile he just stood there and watched Sky approach, not sure what the reaction would be or what Sky would say.

The two men stood there looking at each other and Sky spoke first, asking about Ric's mom and how the world had been treating him during his travels. Ric told him his mother was doing as well as expected, some good days and some not so good days. He told Sky about a few of the places he had been to and the people he had met while traveling.

Ric ventured to ask how Dee was doing and if things had worked out for her and the guy she had been seeing before. Sky told Ric with a big smile that Dee and Vanni were doing great and that they had four children now and were encouraging him to settle down and have a few children of his own.

Ric was quiet and pensive, looking down at his feet as he asked that dreaded question how was Josh. Sky was hoping to avoid the subject because he had some hostility in him still, Mina had not put out all his fire yet.

Sky told Ric that Josh was growing into an awesome young man. That he loved animals especially horses and that he was very intelligent and loved his brothers and sister. He was going to be a science major or work in finance like his father. At this point Sky stopped talking because he noticed the tightness that had collected at the corners of Ric's eyes.

Ric attempted to mask his hurt feelings and said that he was glad that things had gone well for Dee, that she was a wonderful person and deserved nothing but the best that life had to offer. Ric said that he was also happy that Josh was growing into a man to be proud of.

Sky had tried not to think about it, but he was never one for hiding so he had to ask. Sky wanted to know why Ric had never showed up for Josh's christening ceremony. He wanted to know if there had been something more important, but instead of asking he just waited for an answer and watched Ric's face.

Ric simply stated that he did not think he really needed to be there so he went to the pub and had a few beers then went home to sleep as he had an early flight the next day. Sky felt an old familiar emotion coming over him and tried to back away from it, but when he felt his fists tightening up and saw the look on Josh's face he knew he had failed to hide it completely. Sky took a step back to put some distance between him and Ric and then asked his question.

Sky asked if Ric was really telling him that he had no good reason, that he had just ditched his son's christening but before Ric could answer Sky held up his hand and said don't answer that. Sky told him if he answered and the answer was nothing more substantial than what he had just said, a part of him that he had worked hard and long to control may make an appearance that would not bode well for Ric.

At that point Sky turned and walked away very quickly before he changed his mind and became the Sky he was years ago. He could not take a deep breath and his vision was blurry. He kept walking till he got to his truck, got in and drove away a little faster than he should have.

How could someone care so little about their own child that they could ditch their christening, Sky was not the most religious person but he knew God had a place in everyone's life, Libby had taught him that and many other things that had laid the foundation for him to build a better life.

Right now that better life lived in a ranch style house across the lake from his sister and that was where he wanted to be, needed to be more than anywhere else in the world. Except maybe at Libby's feet, which was no longer an option. When his vision blurred again he thought it was the rain falling on his windshield, then he realized it was the tears falling from his eyes.

He would go see Mina and he would feel better. Before Sky could get to the turnoff to Mina's side of the lake his cell phone rang and it was Garvey asking him to meet with him in half an hour. Now Sky was edgy and knew it would take that long to get to *Resolutions*. Damn. He would go see Mina afterwards and maybe he would be able to tell her all the things he had been thinking. Maybe.

Chapter Fifteen...

Greed Hunts For Its Prey

Jeremiah had always been told that patience was a virtue, but he always thought that those words were religious ramblings. Now he had a newfound respect for the religious hypocrites that had spawned him. His vengeful desires had been all that he had to keep him calm when he had spent day after day watching Mina with that man. He had started having dreams of himself, that man and his favorite hunting knife.

He could not imagine what Mina saw in him, and he also could not understand why they had to be together every day. He had spent so much time following them around that he had learned the entire town and the woods around the lake where Mina lived. Jeremiah had no idea where that man lived, but he knew that every opportunity that he had he was at Mina's place. It was almost as if he was purposely trying to keep Jeremiah from his precious girl. Not going to happen.

Jeremiah had taken to hiding in the woods near Mina's house and watching her from there because that sheriff had begun paying too much attention to him and that was not good. He could not afford a run in with the man this close to accomplishing his goal. Nothing good would come of anyone attempting to come between him and Mina as he had already proven.

Jeremiah had become so determined that he was not eating and barely sleeping. When he did allow himself to sleep his dreams were fraught with images of either him and Mina together or him disemboweling that man that would not stay away from his Mina. So sleep was fast becoming as big a negative as driving around town.

Jeremiah was tired of waiting and he had decided that opportunity was not going to come willingly, so he was going to force it to bend to his will as he did everything else. He packed up everything that he had and placed it in the 5th vehicle that he had stolen since his departure from prison. He was going to see Mina and let her know that he had come to get what was his, her.

The dark gray clouds seem to gather in the sky as if they knew what he was about. The pending storm announced its arrival with bright spears of lightning and angry claps of thunder that almost made Jeremiah's ears ring.

Even the forest was in cahoots to hinder his mission, so much so that he had had to create landmarks from his camp to Mina's home to find his way there and back. Almost as if the elements and the environment plotted and planned to thwart him, the downpour of rain attempted to drive him back to his camp and hide his precisely designed landmarks. But Jeremiah had waited as long as the frail tether of patience he held could bare, it was time to have what he came for. What he had lain awake at night in prison thinking about, what he had wanted so desperately that he had almost been able to taste. His Mina was a few feet ahead and he could barely contain his excitement.

He made his way through the woods to Mina's house, he could not figure out for the life of him why someone would build a house with the front door facing the woods. But this whole town had seemed backwards to him since his arrival weeks ago. But he cared not for the ridiculous town or its inhabitants, his only concern was the woman that it had sheltered and for that reason alone he would attempt to leave it somewhat intact.

But the man named Sky would not survive because he had committed the gravest of errors and that was coming between Jeremiah and his Mina and for that he would die. Heaven help him if he had touched her, then he would die slowly and she would be afforded the gift of watching.

Jeremiah made his circular approach to Mina's house almost blinded by the rain, but sheer will and desire drove him to her front door, where he waited and watched. Usually he hid behind the great tree to the left of her front door, but lighting had chosen that very tree just moments before he arrived. Of all the trees in the yard, it had chosen to devour the very one he used as cover; no matter he was tired of waiting and hiding. Jeremiah took the downed tree as a sign that his wait was to end tonight.

Jeremiah paused at the burnt remains of his former hiding companion to scan the area around the house and the dirt road that lead to Mina's backdoor which he could not see. As he was one last time scanning the yard he saw a dark shadow trudging up the road headed straight for the back door. Damn, that man for always getting in the way, he would definitely die slowly and painfully this night.

As Jeremiah fumed with an anger of such heated intensity that it caused steam to rise from his body. How dare he show up now, on the night Jeremiah was planning Mina's great surprise. The storm had already ruined his nice suit that the storekeeper had unknowingly donated, now this idiot of a man was attempting to usurp Jeremiah's ultimate surprise arrival.

While Jeremiah stood there trying to reign in his anger and regain some measure of control Sky approached Mina's backdoor. The anger he felt must have been mirrored by the storm because a huge bolt of lightning lit up the world. No sooner than Jeremiah decided that he would go around the back and confront the interloper, he heard a scream from inside the house and then a scantily dressed Mina burst out the front door barefoot stumbling into the woods in the opposite direction from his camp. Damn, damn, damn that man was as good as dead.

Chapter Sixteen...

A Meeting of the Minds

Bradley had been given a clean bill of health by the orthopedist and told he only needed to use the cane till his balance was better and then he could walk without it. Bradley felt great, the olive branch had been extended to Mel and she had accepted it, hesitantly but still accepted it. He had finished all the court appointed anger management sessions at *Resolutions* and was working again. His boss was glad to have him back and told him that he could see the change and thought it was an excellent improvement.

One last goal to accomplish, Bradley had to meet the guy that Garvey wanted him to work with part time at *Resolutions* and he was 15 minutes early for that meeting. Bradley wore his best Sports jacket and smile as he walked through the door, he had been on time for few events in his life but never early. Today was special and he knew his life was about to change forever.

Alexander and Garvey were waiting for Sky when he walked into *Resolutions*. Alexander was distracted by the two women leaving for the evening, but Garvey noticed the tightness of Sky's shoulders, the heat and intensity in his eyes as well as the redness around his eyes. Garvey was on immediate alert because the last time this man cried someone ended up with a busted nose and two black eyes. Maybe tonight was not the night for this meeting to take place. The two men that were meeting tonight had history and although one of them was longer in the Anger Management program than the other, his present state did not suggest tonight as a good night for the kind of surprise that was coming.

Garvey turned to Alexander and was about to tell him that tonight might not be a good night for this meeting, when Alexander turned to him and started saying the exact thing Garvey was thinking. Both were too late, because as they began speaking at the same time the door swung open and Bradley hobbled in on his cane with his best smile in place, that is until he saw Sky.

Time froze as the four men stood there watching each other like the hunted watches the hunter. Then Bradley closed the distance between himself and the other three men, as he got closer he purposely switched his cane to his left hand and reached out his right to shake hands with Sky.

All Bradley said was Sky's name and shook his hand when Sky reached out his hand. As Bradley's smile widened all the tension just left the room like a child who knows that adult conversation is about to take place so it's time to go.

Garvey pulled up chairs and the four men sat down to talk. What was supposed to be an introductory meeting for Sky and Bradley, quickly became an instant boy's reunion. Everyone knew each other so no one needed to be introduced, each had history with the other so there was no need for background information, each one had their own reason for being there so explanations were not needed, required or expected. Instead they spent an hour or so catching up. Bradley thought he would leave the questions about Dee for another time, Sky was calmer than when he had first entered the room, but not in a place to be interrogated about his sister.

Although Bradley did not know Sky that well, a blind man would have sensed the tension in Sky and Bradley was in no condition to defend himself and he had no desire to be in a position to have to.

The four men decided on a plan and worked out the details, they scheduled their next meeting and stood to leave. As everyone shook hands and stated their excitement about the next meeting and working together, Bradley turned to Sky and put his hand on the other man's shoulder so Sky would have to look at him. Bradley told Sky what he had been thinking since this meeting was scheduled weeks ago, he told him thank you for helping him get his life turned around. If it had not been for that fight in the gym he would have gone through life with a very different mindset.

Bradley told Garvey that he wanted to thank him also for the opportunity to do for others what he and Alexander had done for him, he then reached into his jacket and handed Garvey the check for fifteen thousand dollars to help purchase the new exercise equipment that he knew Garvey wanted so badly.

Bradley said goodnight and left the other three men knowing that he was not the same man that had entered *Resolutions' Anger Management Program* 14 weeks ago and had no desire to ever be that man again or to see him, even in the mirror. He got into his favorite blue corvette and went to meet his sister for what he hoped would be the first of many dinners just to chat and catch up.

As Sky left the center the thunder was rolling louder than before his meeting and the rain was coming down a little harder. He was glad for his favorite hooded army jacket that he always kept in the truck. He hoped Mina was home because he realized now after these two very emotional meetings that he needed to spend some time with her to calm down and center himself.

He drove down to the dirt road turnoff to Mina's and could see nothing but mud, so he decided that he would walk the remainder of the way to help compose his thoughts. Also save himself having to dig his truck out of a mud filled pothole.

He knew he would be drenched when he got to the door but he would rather be wet and focused, than to be dry, angry and frighten Mina.

Sky noticed that Mina had been tired and jumpy the last few weeks and he wondered if she was having as much trouble sleeping as he was. Maybe it was something they should talk about. Just as Sky stepped up on the porch and looked in through the screen door lightning flashed and Mina screamed as if she had seen her own death. Sky snatched the door off its hinges and stormed in the house, just as Mina took off running in the other direction. Why in the world would she run from him, why was she screaming and what had frightened her. Sky was totally perplexed and asking himself questions as he ran behind Mina, he had to protect her and keep her safe because he needed her to live so that he could.

Chapter Seventeen...

Ashley Meets the Real Jason Toliver

Ashley parked her car and wondered why her husband had parked his SUV in the driveway. For more than three weeks now things had been strange between them, ever since her little slip by the pool with Amber her husband had been distant and cold towards her. Amber she had expected to be upset but even April avoided her. Tonight she would have a lovely dinner made and they would sit, eat and be a family like they were before all this happened. She would help them all see it was just a misunderstanding and that they were all fine.

Ashley entered the house and immediately knew something was wrong. April was sitting on the stairs in her favorite jacket with her purple bunny tucked under her arm. April only took her travel bunny when they went on long car rides because it made her feel better to have it along.

Ashley had never liked the idea but her husband thought it was something that she would grow out of eventually so there was no harm in allowing her to carry it when she needed too. Ashley thought it best not to argue, her husband was not a very smart man but he made sure that her and the girls had everything that they needed and wanted, he indulged them all without limits and she was never asked to work or have any more children or anything that she found distasteful so she had learned not to complain or nag him.

Jason Richmond Toliver was one of those rare finds in a man, he just wanted to work at his expensive little calculator and play with the girls.

He was strange like all the corporate accountants she had met at his office, but he loved her girls and was good to all of them. He never required a lot of her so being married to him was rather easy. He was tall and handsome with a nice body and would try some of the things she wanted in the bedroom. She was more adventurous than he was, but Ashley suspected that was because of his limited intelligence. They got along well and life was good. He was wealthy, she was comfortable, there was no prenuptial agreement and she was not expected to function as a broodmare so her life was good.

She had been so relieved when he told her he did not want more children. She had spent the last few years dieting and working out like a fiend to get her body back and had no desire to lose it again to another baby.

Her life was different than she had thought it would be especially after the Charles incidents but, she had made the best of it. They had hit a bump in the road with the events by the pool but she could fix it, if Jason would just stay home till the girls were in bed.

He was a man after all and all men worked the same way, problem was Jason would not touch her or allow her to touch him till the girls were in bed and well asleep. She would ensure that this occurred tonight.

Ashley removed her Cashmere sweater and draped it over the chair, she had always loved the feel of nice things and Jason was great at giving nice and expensive gifts.

She slowly climbed the few steps to approach April and prepared herself for that frightened look that had been her constant welcome recently whenever she got near her youngest daughter. April looked up and watched her the way mother lions watch hyenas when there are new cubs. Ashley spoke softly and quietly to her daughter as she inquired about her jacket and travel bunny. April informed her that daddy Jason was taking them on a trip and mommy was not going. With this April stood up, descended the stairs with the grace of a princess and walked toward the kitchen.

The charm and mature elegance of April's exit had so flattered Ashley, that the child's comment about them going on a trip without her had completely escaped her notice. Ashley was too focused on her thoughts to realize what had been said, she was off to the kitchen and then to see Jason who she knew would be upstairs.

Ashley headed to see cook, she had to ensure that their meal was prepared a little early to guarantee her plans for this evening went off without a hitch.

Upon leaving the kitchen, Ashley heard Amber whispering to someone. Ashley climbed the stairs and met the stare of her oldest daughter Amber. Here was where she really must tread carefully. She spoke to her daughter about her backpack and asked why she was carrying it and her destination. Amber stood there watching her like a mouse watches the cat outside its hole in the wall. When no response came from the girl Ashley felt her patience slipping, so she called her name and asked if Amber had heard her question. Amber still did not answer but Jason did from the top of the stairs. Ashley looked up to see Jason wearing one of his jogging suits that he liked to wear when he was driving.

One of the things that Ashley loved about her life was that everything was predictable. She knew what time her Jason would be home, what time dinner was to be served, when she was to have her hair and nails done; she knew that her girls like to have certain foods for dinner and made sure they had them. She also knew there were particular items that they carried with them when they went on long drives or road trips just as Jason had certain attire he liked to wear when he went on trips. Strange that, because he said nothing about them going on a trip this morning. And April's comment had not made a reappearance to Ashley's mind to give her the warning that it should have, that her plans had been vetoed for the evening and the weekend.

Jason stated that he and the girls were going to his parent's house for the weekend. Ashley was a little confused but managed to recover quickly and stated that she would have a bag packed and be ready in just a few minutes. Jason passed her at the bottom of the stairs and stated that she was not going. Ashley did not recover as well, this time.

Jason noticed that she was having some difficulty understanding what he was saying to her. Something that he had often noticed, but saw no need to draw attention to, that is until now. Jason then instructed one of the nannies to walk the girls out to the car and assure them that he would be along shortly. No sooner than the door had closed, Jason turned to Ashley and said that they were leaving for the weekend, to allow her time to get herself together. Ashley stood staring at the tall beautiful stranger like a deer in headlights.

When she recovered her wits, she inquired as to why she was not allowed to go, Jason looked her in the eye and said, "I've always known that you were not very bright; but you were sweet, beautiful and did not require very much attention so I dealt with it. But now you have turned into this whining angry monster that abuses her children because they love their family and friends more than you." Jason proceeded to tell Ashley that she had four days to decide if she wanted to stay married or not, because he would not continue to live with someone that terrorized the whole house because they were spoiled and unhappy. All Ashley could do was stand there and stare at him. Jason shook his head and walked toward the door.

Just as he reached the door, Ashley's muddled thoughts cleared and she found her voice. She told him that he could not take her girls anywhere without her permission. The second the words left her mouth she regretted them. Especially as Jason walked back to her and the look on his face suggested that maybe she was not as smart as she thought she was.

Jason looked down at Ashley and not so gently reminded her that he had adopted Amber and April, therefore they were his girls as well as hers; and if she continued to behave as she had for the past few weeks, he would leave her, take the girls and dissolve her fantasy life and put an expedient end to the lie that they had been living from inception. Jason then strolled out the door and closed it gently, leaving Ashley standing in the foyer blinking like an owl.

Chapter Eighteen...

We Begin Again

Bryson Alexander had spent so many years as a police officer that he almost did not remember what his life had been like before he became one. He had been eager to grow up and become the man that his father had been. As he stood looking at the pictures that lined the mantle over the fireplace, the very place his mother had put them, he was reminded of different points in his life. Places where he made choices that had helped him as well as hurt him. Pictures of his father in uniform and his mother as well. Both his parents had taught him the art of serving, protecting and putting others first.

His mom had been a nurse at St Michael's Hospital for so many years that when the hospital opened its state of the art cancer unit, it was named for the woman that gave cancer the best fight ever.

The Bethany Alexander Cancer Unit was a regular recipient of major donations and grants that had been initiated by his mom. She loved fundraising for a good cause and was a dedicated volunteer to any event that needed a good cook and strong voice to support it.

His father had been a police officer and had actually served seven years as police captain before he gave it up to come home and take care of his wife and son. His mom had died while he was away at summer camp and that had been hard on him, but his father had helped him deal with it and not hate himself for not being with her. His father had made him see that it was better for her, because women never liked being seen when they did not look their best. At 13 it had seemed reasonable and somehow the way his father explained it, the whole thing made sense. Now he could not imagine how he fell for it.

His father had lived long enough to see him become the next generation in what he thought was the best police force in the world. He often asked himself if his parents would have been proud of him and his life.

Alexander as he was called by everyone including his parents, was looking at the faces throughout his history and his ancestry and he had to ask himself if he had done enough, given enough and could he stop now because he so wanted too.

He had promised himself that once he found a way to make life better for those two sad innocent faces that he still carried in his wallet, that he would leave the force and walk away. He kept that picture of Dee and Sky behind his shield because it was a constant reminder of all the things his parents had taught him were important and vital to life.

He had even spoken to Garvey about his feelings and Garvey had assured him that he would have plenty of work for him now that *Resolutions* had gotten that new contract with the high school and the Scared Straight Program. He had actually been talking to Garvey about it years before when the drinking had gotten him into several come-to-Jesus meetings with the captain.

Alexander had been on a slow downhill slide. He was accused of "use of unnecessary force" on more than one occasion and the nights of drinking too much to dull the pain of losing his father didn't help his attitude.

All the hard work to be the youngest person to make lieutenant, was nearly destroyed because he could not balance life and work without them both reminding him of all he had lost. He wanted to just quit.

Garvey had told him that if he quit then, he would hate himself so he had stayed on the force. Then he had met the Stephens' children and his life had changed and so had he. Alexander fell into a full out love affair with old scotch. They met nightly and stayed close till the wee hours of the morning, neither allowing the other to feel ignored. They were always joined by the image of those two children in his head.

The train that he had climbed under was speeding toward an inevitable crash until the captain put him on a leave of absence, which he had planned to never return from. But Garvey would not allow him to wallow in scotch and depression. He had become the test pilot in Garvey's alcohol rehab program. One might say it was a success because he had since gotten four awards from the department and had not had a drink in 12 years.

Problem was he returned from leave to walk into a gym and see those children grown into teenagers with the same sad, angry eyes. He knew then he had to be better in order to help them get better. With Garvey's help he had done all that and more. Dee was married and happy with children. Sky was rehabilitated to the point he had fallen in love, but he did not recognize it yet.

Now he wanted to do something different. He wanted to spend more time with that cute little blonde that was always having coffee alone every morning. He could not imagine why Erica would be having any time alone, especially breakfast.

He wanted to have her tell him why she looked so sad when she spoke of her father and angry when it was her mother. They had been on a few dates, but now he wanted more. He enjoyed his time at *Resolutions* and had brought several young men and women to Garvey that had been on the verge of a horrific end. They had been able to help them and he wanted to continue that.

91

Alexander knew Garvey had plans to expand the programs that *Resolutions* offered. They had spoken about it often over the last few years and that Garvey wanted to bring more staff on board so that he could offer a full range of classes.

Garvey wanted a Tai Chi instructor, he wanted his former secretary to offer financial instruction, he had desires to bring on 2 or 3 personal trainers. Garvey wanted *Resolutions* to be a holistic environment for those that needed it and provide a positive, productive contribution to their community. Alexander had long desired to be more involved in that process and he had never told Garvey that he planned to contribute financially as well by donating half of his inheritance to the center and its programs. He knew his parents would have done that if they were still with him. Besides he knew that between his investments, his retirement from the military and the modest salary that Garvey would force him to take; he would have more than enough to live comfortably for years to come.

Strange how when you really wanted something, your mind had a way of working it out and revealing all the options so plainly. Not only did he want this, he knew he needed it. Nothing left but to put it in motion. Garvey would help with that part too.

Having Garvey around had been what held him together after the military, after the death of his father and after almost decimating his career. After meeting the Stephens children and getting over his love affair with alcohol and now that he wanted off the force.

They had always talked often and not just about the program or the center participants. They had been in the military together and although they never spoke about that time in their *Special Ops* unit, they did refer to how well they had gotten to know each other during that time. So it was no surprise that he had brought it up to Garvey about leaving the force.

So many bridges in his life had been crossed with Garvey at his back, this one would be no different. He knew Garvey would support his decision, he was just not sure his dad would have. Best to focus on what his mother had taught him and that was to follow his heart.

So many people use to come and talk to his mom about things that he thought the preacher should be jealous. But his mom was a great listener and she often said that that was mostly what people wanted and needed.

Boy, did he want his mom to listen to him right now. Just as the thought crossed his mind, his eyes fell on the photo of him in his father's arms being kissed by his mom. A picture he had looked at often over the years, especially when things got tough. He knew then in that moment that his parents would want his happiness and would understand his desire to leave the force.

So his next stop was to take the letter he had written to the police chief that had been trained by his dad all those years ago. He would let him know that in six months he was done. Done with the force and on to the next phase of what he hoped would be as gratifying as the last.

Chapter Nineteen...

Unconditional Love

Garvey sat at his desk contemplating the phone call that he was about to make. He knew it was necessary, but part of him felt a little like he was playing daddy to two people that really needed a spanking or a good long time out. But he told himself that the time out had already happened and it had lasted way long enough. Bradley needed his sister just as she needed him. They were the only family each other had and there was no reason to allow the suffering to continue.

Because Bradley had listed his sister Melody as his emergency contact, her information was available to Garvey and he wanted her to know what type of man her brother really was and was still on his way to becoming. Not the hot-headed idiot that had wheeled into his center 16 weeks ago with so much anger and hostility that it literally boiled in the air around him.

Garvey and Bradley had talked a lot and he knew about the relationship between them, he also knew that Bradley was sure he had destroyed that relationship with his behavior. Garvey knew firsthand that angry people often did stupid things and then regretted them. Had experienced and witnessed that more than he wanted to admit. Yes this was a phone call he was going to enjoy but it was not going to be easy, but his life had never been and this center and its continued growth and success was proof that difficulties had purpose.

Garvey called Melody and explained who he was and why he was calling. Melody was reluctant to have anything to do with Bradley, but Garvey expected that and was prepared to handle it. One of Garvey's best talents was that he was persuasive. His mom had often told him that he could talk the ants into giving up their queen. After a ten minute conversation with Garvey, Melody was not only on board with his plan she was happy, excited and laughing with him and could not wait to meet him. He knew that would be short lived once she actually saw him as was always the case with women. They loved his voice on the phone, but once they met him there were so many reasons to go the other way that he never really knew which one to blame.

Garvey watched the lightning flash across the darkening sky as he called Alexander and left him a message that the plan was in play. He thought that would make the man smile and get him out of his bag of emotions. Alexander had been in his head for a while lately and it was hard to watch his friend struggle so Garvey picked up the phone and made another call that would make someone's day. This call was just plain interference but Garvey paid no mind to his conscience that often spoke to him with his mother's voice. This call, just like the first one needed to be made. As Laura Jane Garvey would say, "Someone has to do it and God gave you the gift of words so it may as well be you."

The phone was answered on the second ring and he got the usual giggle that his voice always brought out of his little pink tiger. She was a petite little ball of fire and brooked no nonsense from anyone, except him. There had never been a sexual attraction but they had always been able to make each other laugh. She had been his secretary for a few years back before he opened the center and he had tried to hire her but she said that she thought it would be too much of a distraction for the participants and he soon learned she was right. But the friendship had remained intact and she would help him out from time to time and he knew she needed a friend as much as his buddy did. Not to mention they really liked each other.

Garvey smiled as he heard the water splash and knew she was sitting in the tub drinking wine as was her routine way to relax. He had teased her that she was going to get drunk and drown in that tub. He told her what was going to be happening at the center in two weeks and asked her to come and she agreed to do anything for a friend. They talked about the weather and such for a few minutes. Then she told him he was causing her to ignore her lovers, he laughed and told her that wine and bath water did not count as lovers and hung up laughing. True friends were rare and he would do much for his, so he was glad that he could give two really good men a chance at happiness with women they cared about.

There was one other person that weighed on his mind that day but that one was making his on way to love, finally. From the moment Alexander had introduced him to Sky, he had been fond of the young man. There was so much about him that had been Garvey at his age. He wanted to show him everything that he had learned over the years about letting anger take over and run your life. He had spent more one on one time with Sky than anyone other than Alexander.

For the first time in more years than he could remember, Garvey was starting to feel a part of a family. He had Alexander who was more than a brother and now even though he had never spoken it to anyone not even Alexander, he had Sky who he loved as deeply as a son. So much that he was thinking of offering him a partnership in *Resolution*.

Garvey continued staring out the window at the building storm and thought about what his friends would say about his making decisions for them. He realized that in the end they would both make the best use of the opportunities that would come from his recent phone calls.

As Garvey sat quietly thinking about one of his favorite protégés, he had an urge to call Sky and see what was up with him, as the thought went through his mind lightning flashed again and he caught a strange chill at the base of his neck.

All his years in the military had taught him many things and one of which was not to ignore warnings and that chill was just that, a warning and he would do as he had promised himself he would do after he lost his hand. He would never again ignore a warning, awful things happened when you did.

Chapter Twenty...

Mina's Past Out the Closet

Not able to sleep, not even with the extra strength sleeping pills could Mina rest. Mina got up to pace. She always felt better and her thoughts were more organized when she was moving.

How could something that happened so long ago, still have the ability to chase her from her sleep? Again. For the last few weeks, every night she woke up sweating and screaming. The dreams were back, or had they ever really left.

It had always been her plan to make things right but time had been her enemy. Her therapist would always say that time heals everything but it never worked out that way. All these years she had planned to say to her mother that she was sorry; to tell her sister that it wasn't her fault things had gone the way they had; but she had never gotten the chance. Now all she had were the dreams.

Nightmares that would always surface just when she thought she was safe. Or maybe the dreams were her minds' way of letting her know she would never be safe, not as long as he was alive. Alive and angry with her.

Mina stood at the window and stared out. She let the voices of the storm take her back to a place she dreaded going. Mina had been ten years old when the nightmares began. She stood there trapped in the memory with no more control now than she had when it all began. She could remember when the nightmares started just as she remembered when they stopped.

Her mother and father had divorced when she was seven and she thought life was over. She loved her father and he loved his little 'ladybug'. That was the nickname he had given her because of the stuffed toy that always remained in her arms. Her parents had never told her the reason for the divorce but it had been easy to figure out that it had something to do with Jeremiah Senior. He had worked with her mom and she was always different after she had been around him and when he was near her.

Emilee smiled the whole time he was around and he became a permanent fixture a week or so after her dad moved out of the house. Him and his daughter Grace.

Grace was shy and quiet but she was pretty. Grace had been very excited to have another young person around to talk too.

Grace had changed very quickly from a nice, quiet, shy little girl to a whole other person when Mina was around all the time. Somehow Grace thought Mina was going to go live with her dad, but Jeremiah vetoed that idea stating that Grace needed company her own age and that it would be great for both of them. Mina assumed that the change was because she was younger than Grace and could not do all that Grace could do and did not know all the things that Grace knew. But the truth ran to something much more sinister.

Jeremiah had been married before but never discussed his wife, or their marriage but he was very close to his daughter Grace. Initially Mina was envious of the time that Grace spent with her father because no matter how much time Mina spent with George it was never enough. She dreamed often of what her life would be like if she could live with him like Grace had Jeremiah.

Within a month Jeremiah and Grace had moved in with Mina and Emilee. Mina's life and happy childhood memories were over.

Grace disliked her from the moment they moved in and did not hide it except when Jeremiah and her mom was around.

By her eighth birthday, Jeremiah was coming into her room almost every night. When the visits began he had always been drinking or seemed to be drunk.

Mina very quickly learned that the alcohol had nothing to do with the why of the visits, but was merely an excuse for her and her mother's benefit.

Jeremiah married her mother and wanted to adopt her but Mina's father did not like him and because he was still very much a part of her life did not allow the adoption. This was used by Jeremiah as a reason to argue with her mother, because he felt like she should have forced the issue with Mina's father, so that they could be a family.

Two years of fondling and kisses almost every night that made Mina feel like Listerine was the world's best invention, was giving Mina more and more reason to dislike life and miss her father. The weekends that she would go visit her father would always begin and end the same. With her mother and Jeremiah arguing and Grace glad that she was leaving for two days.

Just before her tenth birthday Mina's mom was offered a new job that not only required her to work more nights, but to travel as well.

Two weeks after her tenth birthday Jeremiah told Mina he had a special present for her and she would get it that weekend. Her mom was going out of town for a conference and Grace had a sleepover with friends from her old neighborhood. Somehow Mina knew this was not the kind of present she would enjoy and dreaded the coming weekend.

Emilee thought it would be too much for Jeremiah to handle the girls alone for four days so she called Mina's dad and left him a message about the conference. That Thursday he called and asked for Mina. Her dad apologized for missing her birthday and wanted her to come to his place while her mom was away so he could make up for her missed birthday, Mina was so excited she did not notice that Jeremiah was watching her closely; but Grace did.

The fact that Jeremiah had been spending so much time with Mina had only escaped Emilee's notice, not Mina's and not Graces' and she was angry. Grace felt that Mina was taking her dad from her and was taking her place in Jeremiah's life.

As Mina talked to her dad on the phone she happen to notice the look in Graces' eyes and turned to follow them to Jeremiah's face as he watched her. So startled by the look on both their faces, Mina lost track of what her dad was saying and he had to call her name twice to get a reply from her.

Later her father would say to the police that when he realized that Mina was distracted and had not answered his question about their trip to the zoo, he asked her what was wrong and Mina's reply had put the type of fear and anger in him that lead to murder.

Mina's dad quickly told her he had to go but that he loved her and would always protect her. Mina was so startled by the look on Jeremiah's face that most of what her dad had said went unnoticed until much later.

As Mina attempted to hang up the phone, it took two tries before she got it back in the cradle, her father was on the other end calling her mom leaving her a voicemail that he would be picking Mina up in the morning and taking her to school. George tried to ignore what Mina had said in her absent-minded response but it would not leave his mind.

George knew that Mina had changed but he always assumed it was because of the divorce and her mother remarrying, then he started talking to the therapist that he had started seeing trying to deal with his own feeling and she made it clear that she did not agree with his assessment of the situation regarding Jeremiah Senior and his daughter, now he knew she had been right all along. George decided that he was not going to wait till morning, he was going to get his little ladybug right now and do whatever he needed to do to protect her from everyone.

Jeremiah asked Mina about the call and had to repeat the question twice more before Mina had enough wits about her to answer. His face was really weird and she was all of a sudden deathly afraid of Jeremiah Senior and his daughter Grace.

George ran two stop signs and three red lights on his way to get Mina, but he felt like his life depended on his getting there tonight and could not let his mind wander to the why of it. He arrived at the house with his heart beating in his throat, unsure of what might greet him but he could not let this night pass with his baby girl in that house with that man.

George rang the doorbell and as he waited shifting restlessly from one foot to the other he heard the running of little feet and knew they belonged to Mina, he also heard yelling coming thru the upstairs bedroom window. George leaned out to look up and then he saw a pair of eyes staring at him from another window.

The eyes held anger, fear, hatred and a myriad collection of emotions that should not be coming thru the eyes of one so young. That must be Grace, Jeremiah's daughter and he immediately felt angry and sorry for her, but none of that outweighed his feelings for his own daughter that was standing in the doorway crying because she was so glad to see him.

He opened the door and grabbed his baby girl and almost did not wait to tell anyone he had her, but her mom came to the door looking sleepy and tired. She wanted to know why he was so early picking up Mina, he told her I had too. That he missed her. Mina's mom and Jeremiah did not want Mina to miss school but George told them he would take care of it. He picked up Mina and walked off the porch leaving the bag she had packed and the sad, angry little eyes in the window far behind.

George knew that he was taking Mina away from that place for good, he did not know at that exact moment how he would accomplish such a feat but he would damn well figure it out.

Mina's dad had taken her straight to his therapist's office for a "little chat" and it was revealed what had been happening to her and what Jeremiah was probably planning for the girl. The police were notified and he was arrested. Grace never spoke to anyone and refused to stay with Mina's mom while her dad was gone away. Her aunt came to pick her up a few days after Jeremiah was taken to jail and Mina went to live with her dad.

When she had been questioned by the police, it seemed strange how her mother had no idea why Jeremiah had been so okay with her working nights and leaving him home alone with the girls. Emilee said that Jeremiah was a great supporter of her and her career and that was why he never complained about the traveling and overnight trips. She denied having any knowledge of his behavior but swore she did not believe it, that Mina had made the whole thing up because she did not want her mom to be happy with anyone but George. Mina later wondered how the police had responded to that, but had no one to ask.

Mina often wondered what Grace told the police when they asked her questions about the things that Mina was saying regarding her father. But Mina had no one to ask about that either.

Mina's mom had never attempted to fight George for custody, but she stayed married to Jeremiah the whole time he was in prison.

Because Emilee felt it would somehow be important to Jeremiah, she had maintained contact with Grace.

Although this was done only by letters and phone calls because Grace always claimed she was active in school and clubs and could not come to visit. Emilee never quite believed the girl but did not push the issue.

Emilee even tried talking to Grace's aunt and for the first few weeks it went well then all of a sudden Jeremiah's sister became hostile and refused to speak with Emilee, so she would just write to Grace and occasionally get letters in return.

It was only when Grace turned 16 and finally decided to tell Emilee the truth about her relationship with her father that she divorced Jeremiah.

But Grace only told her the truth so that when her dad was out of prison she could once again have him all to herself and not have to share him with anyone. Grace still hated Mina and blamed Mina and through her, Emilee for having lost Jeremiah to prison.

Two years later when Jeremiah was out of prison he did not want to see Grace and he did not care about the divorce. All he wanted to know was where George had taken Mina. Because he wanted her back.

He used every resource he had to find them and once he found Mina and George he began sending flowers and notes to Mina.

Over the next five years everywhere they had gone, Jeremiah would find them. Her father tried everything he could to get the police to see that Jeremiah was after his daughter, but he could never prove anything. Then the real monster came. George was diagnosed with liver cancer and died within six of the twelve months he had been given. Mina was alone and began thinking about Grace and how she'd had to grow up without her father. Monster he may have been but he was still her father and she loved him, just as Mina loved George.

Mina had always wanted to tell Grace and her mother that she was sorry for all that had happened. Therapy had finally convinced Mina it was not her fault but she now felt like the three of them were in the same boat, they had all lost a man they loved and it hurt just the same.

Mina told herself that one day she would try to make peace with her mother and with Grace, if for no other reason than they were all the family she had left.

Two years after her father's death the flowers had showed up at their condo. Mina had packed up, sold the condo and moved to the ranch that her father had been repairing in the event they needed to move again. Three weeks ago Mina had come home to flowers on her step and the dreams had begun the next night. It seemed two was not a lucky number for her, for it had only been two years of fragile peace here at the ranch. Now Mina wondered where she would go and would she be able to sell the ranch after all the work they had put into it. Would she ever be rid of Jeremiah Senior and would he ever leave her be.

The day had dawned hours ago, cloudy and dreary a perfect reflection of her current mood. As Mina sat on the arm of the chair staring out at the building storm she heard a knock on the door and turned to look out.

Still entangled in the web of her reverie brought on by last night's dream, her imagination clouded her vision so much so the man in the hooded jacket peeking in the back door made her scream and run.

This time he had done it. Jeremiah had found her, and he would have her because George was gone and there was no one to come and save her.

Chapter Twenty-One...

The Truth Hurts More Than Lies

All those years Maria had spent wishing for an opportunity to speak with Charles. Had she really sat in therapy sessions defending him and accusing her daughter of lying. For years she had actually believed he was innocent and that her daughter was just a mean and vengeful little girl that wanted to further destroy her life. Now with the truth out in the open like a huge nasty bruise on her face, she could no longer hide that Charles really was a monster. That what she had thought was a demented old woman, was really the only person that had cared enough to protect her child when she had failed so miserably.

Libby had been honest and truthful, she had loved Dee so much that the man she had loved as a son did not stand a chance in the face of her beliefs of right and wrong. And oh was he wrong. He had planned and plotted the brutal rape and torture of her very own daughter.

After all the years of friendship. All the hours he had spent sitting and talking to her about their life in college and pretending to entertain her children. All Charles had really been doing was carrying out a vicious plan to do to her daughter what he probably had done to many other little girls.

Now she had to think about that too. How many other children had he terrorized and traumatized for his own sick pleasure. He was a worse animal than the one she had been married to. Strange how seeing Charles for what he really was had also brought to light the truth about Jonathan and totally destroyed the false image of the man she had married.

How could she have missed it? Maria was pacing around her little seaside condo, totally ignoring the gorgeous view out her bay window. She was too caught up in reliving the time before the treehouse incident. Maria had to pull out all the memories of the time after Charles' reappearance in her life to try and find that missed moment when he had shown his true colors and she overlooked it. No amount of reassurance from her husband or anyone else could help her now. She had to own her part in this.

Maria had no desire to revisit her past. No interest in pulling out painful memories to see if she had failed her daughter in such a major way, especially after she had been reminded of how often she had failed others. Then to realize that those failures included her very own children made her stop and stand very still. Why did that thought give her a horrific case of goose flesh on her arms. Maria's eyes began to roam the room looking for an answer as diligently as her mind attempted to gain purchase on that steep slope of realization going on in her befuddled brain. Her thoughts crash landed at the same moment that her eyes fell on the picture of her and Ashley hugging each other at the homecoming parade. The only one Ashley had attended while Maria was away at college. Then the reason for the uncomfortable feeling hit her square in the face.

Ashley. Her sister Ashley had been fascinated with Charles from the beginning, almost from the moment she had met him. Now Maria had to really ask herself what else had she missed. Had Charles done the same evil to her little sister that he had with her daughter.

Was Charles the real reason that her little sister hated her daughter so much that she could not help Maria see reason when the truth had been standing right in front of them both.

108

That a stranger had seen what they both refused to see. Refused for different reasons, but refused nonetheless.

Had Ashley not been able to see it because in her damaged mind she was in love with Charles and thought he was using Dee to make her jealous so she would give him more of what he wanted.

But what else could he possibly want, he had already had her when she was too young to know better and make sense of...Maria stopped cold. Now she knew, the truth went thru her like a spear of ice thru her heart. Amber and April. Had Charles wanted access to her nieces and was her sister's mind clouded enough to allow it. The way Maria had with her own daughter and her little sister. Had Maria really given Charles all the things that made her life worth living, lead them like lambs to be slaughtered.

Maria wanted to call her sister and ask that dreaded question but how do you start a conversation like that when you have barely spoken one in three words to your own sister in more than three years. Maria had to face the sad reality that she had not gone to her sister's wedding and that was after she sternly refused to be in the wedding. Even the reason she gave had been sad.

Maria had told Ashley that she did not want to watch anyone destroy their own life like she had with her own. Then two years later Maria had been forced to marry Montgomery without her sister, her mother or her children in attendance. Looking back now, had she been wrong.

Now she had to look at the truth of the matter, that it was not her decision to make if Ashley should marry or not. Not her place to judge anyone's attempt at happiness.

Ashley and Jason had been together for a few years and things were going well as far as she knew and the girls were very happy. She knew this because her son had called to tell her how angry he was that she had ruined his aunt's day by not being supportive of her happiness. That she continued to make everyone suffer for her unhappiness. Maria had attempted to argue with Sky regarding his evaluation of her actions, now she knew that he had been right but for the wrong reasons. She did not envy their happiness but their peace of mind, their ability to live past all the horror and pain. Their willingness to let go of the past and embrace the future like a lost lover come home.

The one thing that did give Maria a bit of calm is that she had followed her gut response that day in the kitchen when she had found Sky standing over Charles.

She had taken the gun from him, because she knew even then that she was responsible for the shooting. Sky may have pulled the trigger but she was the reason that Charles was in their lives, she was at fault; she was really the poison that had killed everything good. In her life and in theirs.

So here was the reason she had needed all the therapy, the reason her ex-husband had brutalized her all those years. Why she never slept well, why she had no relationship with her sister or her mother.

Why her children hated her and why her ex-husband had taken her ability to paint. Why even though Montgomery was trying desperately to love her, she fought it and him every step of the way. She now believed it was punishment because she did not deserve to hold the skill to create beauty when everything about her had caused pain and suffering to everyone she loved. Oh, how awful the truth could be when it showed up at your door; uninvited unwelcomed and undesired. Life was a bit more tolerable when she had been drowning in a sea of lies and could use anger to stay afloat, when her life had coasted along the river of denial. But truth had a way of snatching the rug of deception right out from under you. Leaving you aching and bleeding from all the holes truth can tear open. For once she found herself lying on the floor beaten and she felt she deserved it.

Chapter Twenty-Two...

Age Does Not Maturity Make

Ashley found herself sitting on the stairs lost and confused. This had quickly turned into the worst day of her life, well the second worst day of her life; just as before she was more concerned about people knowing what happened than dealing with what had happened. Just as she was about to get up and go after her husband and her daughters one of the maids brought her the phone. It was her mother asking her if she had talked to Maria because she had not been able to reach her. Of course Ashley had no idea what was going on in Maria's life because Maria did not confide in her anymore nor did they talk on regular basis.

Then her mother asked her what was going on with her and she decided that she would for once be the one to tell her own tale rather than have someone else tell it for her.

As she began telling her mother that Jason had gone to his parents with the girls, she made light of the fact that she had not gone with them. Ashley tried to make it appear that it had been her choice to stay behind. But just as her husband and children were predictable so was she, more than she knew. Her mother asked her what had happened between her and Jason, or her and the girls to make him take them and leave her.

Ashley wanted to feign ignorance and just hang up on her mother, but she was at a low point and she needed someone to tell her how to fix this. So instead of her usual arrogance, Ashley took a deep breath, removed her shoes and began climbing the stairs while she revealed the whole sordid mess to her mother leaving out nothing. No conceit, no attitude, no aloofness just the honest truth mixed with a lot of tears and begging for her mother to explain to her where she had gone wrong.

Sarah Jones was a no-nonsense type of woman that had never coddled her girls and did not mince words. She told Ashley the cold hard truth about herself and how she had been living her life for years.

By the time Ashley had reached the guest bedroom, the only place she could go without seeing her children and her husband everywhere, her mother had laid her bare. She had no intentions of arguing because she knew in her heart and soul her mother was right.

Her mother asked her why she had behaved the way she had and Ashley told her the truth about everything, including the events that had occurred when Maria was away at college. She told her mother that she blamed Dee for everything and that she had told herself that if Dee had not been born that her life would have been different.

Sarah felt sorry for her youngest daughter and fought hard to temper her tone and soften her words because for once she knew her baby girl was in pain and this was her one and only opportunity to reach her.

Sarah told Ashley the real truth about her feelings and encouraged her to be honest with not just everyone else but with herself as well. They talked for another few minutes and Ashley did something her mother never thought in life that she would do, Ashley asked her mother to pray with and for her.

Of course Sarah jumped at the opportunity and through her tears of joy, her and her baby girl cried and prayed together as they had when she was little. They both said joyous and tearful good byes and then hung up.

Ashley lay there replaying her mother's words and realized what she had to do if she wanted to keep what really mattered most to her. She would not lose another minute of her life and she would not continue to blame anyone else.

It was time to grow up and face the real world, ready or not. The first step was her sister, then her niece. After that she would call her husband and her daughters.

When Maria's phone rang she just stood there staring at the object on the table making that shrill noise. She managed to answer it before her machine picked up and was more shocked than she had words for. Ashley started by telling Maria how much she loved and missed her. That she wanted them to spend some time together and that she was not angry about Maria skipping her wedding that she understood.

When the capacity for speech returned to her, Maria asked Ashley what had happened. Ashley gave Maria the scaled down version but the truth about her and Jason and what had happened with the girls and her feelings about her niece. She told Maria that she was facing her demons and attempting to conquer them for the sake of keeping what mattered to her. Maria wanted to fully embrace this new Ashley but before she could she had to face a few demons of her own.

Maria asked Ashley about her time with Charles and if anything had happened between them. Ashley was glad to relieve her sister by telling her that she had just been a stupid little girl and that Charles had laughed at her and sent her home just as he had told her all those years ago. Maria realized in that moment just how fortunate her little sister had really been and how her poor daughter had not.

All the ugly things Ashley had said and thought about Dee came back to haunt her. So much so that she knew a phone call would not solve this, it was time for a visit and she begged Maria to go with her.

Although Maria agreed with Ashley, she was not ready to face her daughter just yet. Ashley told Maria she understood and that it changed nothing, that she still wanted them to have their time but the next day she was going to see Dee. Maria wished her the best, told her little sister that she loved her and said goodnight.

As Maria hung up, she realized that although her sister was the youngest, she was more mature than Maria and had just proved it in spades.

Chapter Twenty-Three...

Crossing Burned Bridges

V anni was awakened by the phone. As he reached to answer it, he took care not to release his hold on Dee as she slept. They had long ago learned that she slept better when he held her and he slept better because his presence seemed to keep the nightmares at bay and she did not wake up screaming.

Ashley listened as her nephew in-law took care to wake Dee gently. As she sat in her daughter's favorite chair the reality of all Dee had suffered came to settle heavily in the room with her. It made her task harder, but so very necessary and no matter what it took she would do this, tonight.

Dee took the phone and said a hesitant hello. There had been very few kind words spoken between her and her aunt Ashley and Dee was not interested in having her feelings and emotions filleted by Ashley especially at this late hour.

Ashley started by apologizing for the lateness of the hour but stated that she could not put off what needed to be said any longer. Initially the sound of Ashley's voice made Dee pay close attention, but the gentle apology made Dee sit up in bed and wonder if she was dreaming the whole thing. But as Vanni turned and shifted her body so that she rested comfortably against his chest as he leaned back against the headboard, made her realize there was too much movement for her to be dreaming as she was a very light sleeper.

As Ashley began explaining the reason for her call and telling Dee all the things that had come to her heart and mind while on the phone with her mother earlier, Dee did not even try to stop the flow of tears. Although he had played referee to many conversations between his wife and her aunt over the years, Vanni realized that tears or not, this was one he was going to have to sit out.

Dee reached over and grabbed his arm and pulled it around her body like she was attempting to use his body as a blanket. He just kissed the top of her head, held her and began to rock her gently as she listened to her aunt speak and continued to cry silently.

When the call was done, Dee said thank you, goodnight and handed him the phone. As Vanni replaced the phone Dee curled into his chest and continued to cry softly.

Vanni asked no questions, just held onto the most precious thing he had ever held except his children. He had never doubted his love for Dee and tried daily to ensure that neither did she.

He never thought to ask the nature of the conversation because his intuition told him this was a conversation just for Dee and Ashley. He also knew that one day it would be just as emotional in the telling.

He held on to the love of his life, rocked her gently and did the only thing he knew how to do. Pray. He prayed the way Libby had taught him all those years ago.

It had always served him well, and even though he had not grown up praying; he had learned the power of prayer and would not hesitate to seek help from God when he needed it as he surely needed it right now. Just as he knew he would surely thank God when this season of turmoil was over.

Chapter Twenty-Four...

The Hunt For Mina

Grace never knew what it was about Mina that made her father act the way he did. He had been immediately drawn to her the first time he saw her. Grace started to reminisce as she drove along following her father's car as he drove two cars ahead. She had become very good at following him without him knowing it. Grace could never say what her point was in following him but she had always loved her father more than anything or anyone in the world and if he was going to do something that would cause him to be separated from her again, then she was going to be there to try to stop him.

Jeremiah had never paid any attention to his rear view mirror, or felt that someone was watching him. His level of paranoia was so high already that nothing else could trigger a reaction from him.

He never saw the woman sitting in the booth four tables over watching him eat. Never noticed the green compact on every bridge and following his every turn. He never heard the soft tread of her leather moccasins in the woods shadowing his every step. Grace had learned to be careful and ever vigilant in following her father around.

Grace had found out about her father's escape from prison from the police that came to her apartment asking questions. She did not have to have anyone tell her where he would be heading or why. Grace knew if her father was out, he would be looking for Mina as he had always told her would. It had been strange when he had refused her visits and her letters for the first two years.

Then one day she receives a letter begging her to come visit, Grace had not been surprised that his only questions about her had been did she know how to use a computer, did she have money saved up and did she drive.

Grace was not surprised, she was angry. Her father was in prison because of Mina and yet he still wanted her, still seemed to need her. Why could he not see that she was right here and would do anything in the world for him if he would just love her the way he had before Mina arrived. Well Grace decided that her father needed help and the only one that could help him was her, so she would. She would help him get the medicine that he needed to heal. Medicine in the form of Amina Laurel, because he had always said that she was a drug he was addicted to.

As Mina had run thru the woods in her bare feet thinking that her worst fear was only a few steps behind her, Grace had stood in the trees and watched her father run into the woods right past her trying catch Mina and keep an eye out for Sky at the same time. She knew he would not stop until he had what he wanted in his grip. She was there for only one reason to make sure that her father got what he wanted and no one hurt him. She was his protection from everyone and everything that posed a threat to him including Mina. Too bad for Mina because she was never going to have Jeremiah, not as long as Grace was around.

Mina was never able to see clearly the man behind her, but she could hear him calling her name, and his heavy footfalls as he ran. She had to find a way once and for all to get away from him, but that would not be enough. She had to also find a way to keep him from coming after her ever again.

Garvey had seen Sky's truck beside the road and went in search of him to make sure he was okay. He knew about Sky's past and he was not willing to let the man he had come to love as a son suffer anymore at the hands of anyone if he could prevent it. He could not shake the feeling that something was off. He had received that warning as thoughts of Sky crossed his mind and always before that meant that person was in need or in danger, so he was going to check on Sky.

Garvey could not tell the precise moment when Sky's presence had taken on epic proportions in his life. Originally he had just wanted to help as he did with all those that came to him. But after a long night of too much vodka and listening to Alexander talk about his experiences with the Stephens children, Garvey had become more than a little curious. He had heard Alexander speak about the photo he carried but had never seen it and never dared to ask. But this night all bets were off and Alexander had voluntarily pulled out his shield wallet and showed Garvey the picture he kept tucked behind his badge. A reminder he said, of what happens when you forget to care. When you need to remember what's important and for him why he woke up and went to work every day. To keep the monsters under the bed and in the closet where they belonged.

Just as with Alexander, Garvey saw something in that photo that fired up his protective instincts and made him want to be better and do more. He had gained a new respect for what his friend endured every day that he was on the job. Had seen firsthand how impossible it was to turn it off. He had met and grown to love and respect the young man in that photo that was somehow stuck in that little boys world, with no one to help him.

No one except Alexander and now Garvey. Because he would do everything in his power to show Sky that all fathers were not like the one he had been born to.

What Garvey saw initially when he pulled into Mina's driveway was the house sitting calmly in the torrent of rain the sky had opened up and down poured on the earth about 30 minutes ago. Although the warning was chiming thru his body he saw nothing to justify its presence, so he was about to turn his truck around and leave. About halfway into his swing around he saw it, Mina's back screen door hanging off its hinges like a bad stripper leaning on a pole she had no idea how to use.

Garvey slammed the truck in park, grabbed his phone and speed dialed the one man he wanted at his back when things got tight. Alexander picked up on the second ring and Garvey did not give him time to inhale he simply spoke in the code language that they had always used, then hung up and left his truck. He did not take his phone because the man that just exited his truck was not the same one that had driven it to Mina's. Garvey was in another mindset and in another place and time.

Sky had no idea who the man was chasing Mina but he had seen several glimpses of him in the woods as he had lost her trail and had to circle back around to find her. He knew whoever he was, he could not have Mina, she was his and that meant he would die to protect her if he had to.

Considering the man was running through the woods with a huge hunting knife in his hand, one of them would definitely have to die, because neither was going to give up easily.

Chapter Twenty-Five...

A Friend In Need

Alexander stripped out of his dress clothes and put on all black gear and grabbed his essentials and was out the door in ten minutes. Garvey had let him know where he was and what he saw. Garvey knew Alexander would draw the necessary conclusions and be at his back in less time than it took for a chicken to cross the road.

Mina was more afraid of Jeremiah than she had ever been because she was alone. No one knew where she was and what was happening to her. She found a fallen tree and tried hide long enough to see where Jeremiah was. She crouched quietly behind the tree trunk trying to see and hear past the wet hair in her face and the sheeting rain. She was trying desperately to see something, anything and could see nothing. Just as she turned to look behind her she was grabbed and held by a hand over her mouth.

Fighting was useless and besides she remembered that Jeremiah liked it when she struggled. As she lay there held tightly in his iron grip, her body relaxed because something was very different about the way he held her. Something about the feel of his body was very different and her mind was trying to tell her that she should be focusing on trying to get away not trying to figure out what was different.

Sky turned Mina in his arms without removing his hand from her mouth because he knew the man was near and he could not afford to have Mina scream and alert him to where they were. As Mina looked up at him and he removed his hood, she threw her entire body at him and held on to him like her life was ending and she wanted to take him with her. She attempted to say something but Sky put a finger to her lips and pointed with his head in the direction that Jeremiah was now standing about 20 feet away.

Just as Jeremiah turned and saw Sky and Mina huddled in the rain beside the tree, Garvey stepped clear of the trees. Jeremiah was headed toward them planning to do great bodily harm to the man holding onto what he felt belonged to him.

Jeremiah was about ten feet away when all of a sudden a man he had seen a few times around town walked in front of him and smiled, but the smile was one of those that would cause a smart man to take a step back.

Sky pushed Mina into Garvey and went to help Alexander, because Sky knew this man was ready to kill to get to Mina and before he gave up he would hurt everyone and anyone to get her. Alexander stood in front of Jeremiah looking like he wanted Jeremiah to charge him, the expression on his face made Sky think that Alexander would much rather kill this man than arrest him. Jeremiah told them this was between him and Mina and none of their concern. Neither Sky nor Alexander said a word just stood there in the pouring rain watching this maniac with a hunting knife the length of Sky's forearm attempt to stare past them at the huge black man attempting to drag a screaming crying Mina in the other direction.

Mina had never known this level of fear. Here was Sky and Jeremiah in a faceoff and Sky was defenseless. Jeremiah had always told Mina that he would gladly kill to get what he wanted and what he wanted right now was her. Mina was perfectly willing to sacrifice herself to protect the man she loved, and loved Sky she did.

Amazing how the truth was always the last one to show up in an intense situation.

The fight ended as quickly as it began. There was a lot of struggling and then Sky was on the ground on his knees holding his stomach and there was blood dripping from the end of Jeremiah' knife. Alexander had attempted to pull his weapon and Jeremiah had sliced the harness right off his shoulder.

Alexander pulled his own blade and with the softest up swing Mina had ever seen sliced into Jeremiah's chest like carving a Thanksgiving Turkey.

As Jeremiah stumbled back, Garvey yelled something at Alexander and he moved in on Jeremiah with his blade held high about to finish what he had started. No sooner than Alexander took his first step forward he spun around like a child's marionette on a broken string and fell to the ground. Garvey shoved Mina in the opposite direction of the fighting and ran toward his friends. For a breath and a second more nothing happened then Jeremiah took a step in her direction and then another, then another and then began to run towards her. Mina turned to run as Garvey had told her minutes before and did not make but two or three steps, because Grace was standing in the clearing behind her holding a big gun.

Mina attempted to sidestep Grace and was yanked backwards by her hair by Jeremiah. As Mina pinwheeled her arms to keep her balance Jeremiah continued to reel her in by her hair. But he never made good on his attempt, because just as he was about to reach out and pull her against him, Grace fired the gun and Jeremiah stared at his daughter in total confusion. He attempted to take another step and Grace fired again. She walked up to Jeremiah as he fell to the ground.

Sky had gained his feet and staggered over to Mina and held her close to him and they both turned to look at the scene playing out three feet away.

Grace stood over Jeremiah and told him that she loved him and that if she could not help him she would not lose him to prison again and then she fired the weapon again. As Jeremiah's body lay on the ground leaking like an old water hose, Grace turned to Mina and told her that she was sorry that she had not protected her sooner.

She told Mina that she had hoped that prison would heal him of his desire for her, but since it had not, that Jeremiah had left her no choice. Then Grace put the gun to her own head and pulled the trigger. Everyone watching yelled at the same time to no avail. Grace's body fell beside her father's.

Sky realized what Grace was about to do and grabbed Mina and turned her face into his chest as he watched the horrendous scene play out because he could not stop it any more than anyone else could have as they were all injured in some way.

His only thought was here he was again with a body lying at his feet, only this time he was not the cause; nor was he concerned about it. He simply put his arm around Mina and walked over to check on his friend and mentor lying on the ground.

Later at the hospital, as he was questioned Sky said very little because there was very little that he knew. As each one of them was questioned, the same became true of them all. No one knew all the details they were simply reacting to a threat in the only way they knew how.

They sat together and waited while Alexander was in surgery having the bullet removed from his chest. When he was in recovery and the police were thru with their questions Sky had a realization. He was back in a hospital waiting while someone he cared about was treated, and his only saving grace was the woman he now held onto. Just as Mina had helped him maintain his sanity when his mother was in the hospital, she gave him solace now as he waited for news of Alexander's condition.

Mina sat there in her wet, bloody clothes wrapped in a blanket and Sky's arms with them both watching Garvey wondering what they were thinking as they watched each other. The surgeon came out and told them that Alexander was going to be fine that the bullet had been removed and that he would be sore for a while but that he would heal and be good as new. Mina wondered would any of them ever be good again.

Garvey walked over to Sky and pulled him to his feet and with the one hand he had, grabbed him in a hard embrace and whispered in his ear then walked away.

As Garvey got a few feet away, Sky yelled behind him, "me too. Me too." Garvey gave him a big smile, stepped on the elevator and waved as he waited for the doors to close.

Sky fell into more than sat in the chair beside Mina and leaned his head back on the wall, he started speaking before Mina realized he was talking to her. He told her that he had been coming to tell her that he loved her and that he had since he had spent weeks reading to her as a child in the hospital. Mina told him that she loved him too. Then she told him that she often wondered if he thought of her and that time so long ago. He told her that he had never forgotten it or her.

She kissed his bruised cheek and told him that the only other man she had ever loved was her father. He grabbed her and kissed her back and that's how Vanni and Dee found them. Dee stopped in her tracks and felt an instant pang of jealousy, then Vanni hugged her and she smiled because she remembered that she had prayed for one thing more than anything else, and that was for her brother to find a love like hers. Watching them, she heard Libby's voice say *God answers prayers*. Of course, Libby was always right.

~ T h e   E n d

Special Thanks.........

To God be the glory. This was a labor of love. Love for everyone that gave something of themselves to help make this book possible. Thank you to all the people who believed and supported me. To my husband, there will never be enough words to say all that you mean to me. A special thank you to my youngest son for playing bodyguard as I sat up way too late to write this book. He made sure I ate and that I did eventually get some sleep. I love you Bugg. To my beautiful daughter, every mother should have one just like you. To all my children, you will never know how much I truly love you. To my sisters, you girls are made of stuff that is forever priceless.

I wish everyone had a Sweetie, a Tay and a Muffinpie but these are mine. I love you all. Remember that family and friends are precious and should not only be told but shown. It's never too late, so if you have not said it; you should say it or at least show it. May God continue to bless you all. As my best friend AT says, remember to **P.U.S.H. Pray Until Something Happens**

Look for the exciting conclusion

Book Three of
The Storm Tales

Where the Rivers Meet

Is one man so important that he can monopolize and continue to control the life of the woman he ruled with an iron fist even after his death?

Or will she finally let go of the past and reach toward the future that lives and breathes without her every single day.